UNSPOKEN MAGIC

AN AGENTS OF MAGIC URBAN FANTASY NOVEL

SARAH BIGLOW

 Created with Vellum

AUGUST 9, 2019

ONE

The sun was just starting to dip below the buildings in downtown as I powered down my computer, exhaustion wrapping itself tight around my body. I'd joined the FBI to help people and live up to Ezri's legacy. I'd managed that, at least according to the people who'd mattered to her, a few months ago when we'd solved the bank robbery case. But since then, the cases had all felt so *mundane*.

"What's that look for?" Agent Duncan, my partner, asked from his seat across the way.

He was a little more than just my partner in the field these days. We'd gone on a date or two. It was nice to be able to talk about magic with someone who had some distance from it while still understanding what I meant. I hadn't intended to spill the beans to him, but it hadn't been possible to keep the cat in the bag when the bank robbery case was so wrapped up in dark magic.

"Nothing," I sighed, rubbing my temples. "Just thinking how the last few cases we worked have felt kind of … tame?"

"Oh, don't go jinxing us," he replied with a laugh. "I mean, you didn't really think there were only going to be magical crimes for us to solve, did you?'

Embarrassment warmed my cheeks. A small part of me had assumed that would be the case. After all, there were plenty of magically inclined criminals in this city. And every time I'd crossed paths with Ezri, she'd been tracking down some magical kidnapper or killer.

"Well, I mean there are literally governing bodies to keep people like me in line. Why couldn't that extend to actual law enforcement?"

He stood and crossed the distance, leaning on the outer wall of my cubicle with one arm. "I guess it's possible. But if you have an entire agency in the know, it kind of defeats the purpose of magic being secret, right?'

I nodded. "I think I'm just grumpy, that's all."

"I know what can fix that." He beamed down at me.

"Beer and bed?" I replied.

"Something like that. Come on," he said, pulling me to my feet.

I cast a glance toward one of the offices situated on either side of the large conference room. Molly had left about an hour ago, but I could still see Jacquie sitting there, bent over her computer.

"Give me a minute," I told Duncan and side-stepped him. Closing the distance to her office, I knocked twice before easing the door open. "We're getting out of here." After a beat, I added, "Do you want to come?"

Jacquie turned from her computer screen and I noted the tired expression on her face. I recognized the sag in the skin under her eyes and the slightly sunken cheeks for lack of sleep and forgoing self-care. I was guilty of that all too often myself. I opened my mouth to retract the invitation when she let out a long breath.

"Sure. I could use a night out."

I did my best to hide my surprise and offered a smile. "We'll meet you in the lobby, then."

She nodded wordlessly, busying herself with wrapping up her work and I retreated to the cubicles.

Duncan loitered by my desk. He'd abandoned the tie and suit jacket, and undone the top button on his shirt. His version of casual.

"Jacquie's joining us," I announced and caught the slight deflation in his expression.

He'd been hoping for a date. I just wasn't up for the intimate small talk required. "I told her we'd meet her downstairs," I noted and started for the elevators.

The security officer stationed at the front desk eyed us uneasily as we waited. Despite the fact I still had my badge and gun clipped to my belt, our continued presence appeared to unnerve the man. Finally, Jacquie arrived. She, too, had left her suit jacket in her office and had changed into a less formal pair of slacks. I felt woefully overdressed as we followed Duncan out onto the street.

"Where are we heading?" Jacquie called as he led us down the street toward Government Center station.

"There's a place I've been meaning to check out," he replied.

My stomach did a flip as we got off at the first Boston University stop on the B line. I could see the long line snaking down the sidewalk outside of the bar Notre Dame. It was not a place I liked to spend time. It brought back too many painful memories. That, and the owner, was kind of a dick who didn't like me.

"Why don't we find somewhere else? This place is going to be way too crowded," I urged, catching Jacquie's eye. I hoped she would back me up. She had her own history with this place thanks to her investigations into magically linked cases with Ezri.

"It's the only magical bar in the city," Duncan protested.

"I know. I've been. It's not that exciting. Pretty boring really. And the drinks suck," I replied.

"Agent Cartwright seems to like them," he mumbled.

"That's because she has a vested interest," Jacquie snorted.

Her words sent a shiver of revulsion down my spine. I knew that Molly and Jonathan—the bar's owner—had been seeing each other off and on, but I did my best to forget that fact whenever possible. I honestly couldn't understand what she saw in him.

I gestured to the long line that wound its way down the block past several storefronts. "It's packed. There's no way we're getting in any time soon," I continued. "And it is way too hot to stand out here waiting."

As if by magic, the front door opened and Molly stepped out into the humid air and spotted us. She leaned in, whispered something to the bouncer, gestured toward us, and the bouncer nodded.

"You three, go on in," the bouncer said in a booming bass tone.

I suppressed a groan as Duncan all but ran inside. I cast Molly an annoyed look, but she only offered a shrug. "He really wanted to check it out," she said over the thrum of the bass as we moved from the front foyer into the bar proper.

"Then maybe you should have taken him with you," I muttered. The ambient noise around us swallowed my retort, which was probably for the best.

We settled at one of the high-top tables situated halfway between the bar and the dance floor. I cast a look around the space and a hint of magic seeped out of me. Being back here triggered my power's instinct to exert its control over me. I didn't fight it this time. Instead, I let it wash over me and it sharpened my senses. I could hear the couple at the far end of the bar bickering over whether he'd had too much to drink. The scent of stale beer and liquor accosted my nose. My gaze narrowed in on a guy with a buzz cut across the dance floor, ripples emanating from his fingertips. They traveled down to the floor, sending the girl dancing near him stumbling into his waiting embrace. His face was sweaty by the time she landed in his arms, like what he'd done took a huge effort on his part. Despite having apparently accomplished his goal, he looked around, as if afraid someone else had noticed what he'd done.

Jonathan detested the use of magic in his bar, no matter the reason. He especially despised people using it to hurt others. Which was kind of ironic given how fucking scary the man could be when he wanted. My body, infused with my own power, allowed me to move double speed unseen across the floor. A sudden nauseous feeling hit me the moment I stopped moving and a strange unease wrapped around me. A voice in the back of my head told me I shouldn't have done that. It wasn't like the few sips of alcohol I'd had could have done this. No, this felt like someone else had gotten in my head. The voice sounded eerily like Jonathan.

I tried to ignore the feeling and pulled the girl free of the man's groping fingers.

"Back off," I snapped, putting myself in his way.

His face blanched as he gave me a once over and he beat a hasty retreat, shoving other patrons out of his way in the process. I looked down only to realize I'd forgotten to take off my badge and holster. Maybe

I wasn't as overdressed for the evening as I'd first imagined.

"You done scaring the locals?" Jacquie quipped as I returned to the table.

"Just doing my civic duty," I replied, noticing Duncan's absence.

"He's getting drinks," Jacquie filled in, reading my confused expression.

From my new vantage point, I had a clear view of the bar. I spotted a young woman manning the bar who I recognized as Jonathan's niece, Missy. I must have stared longer than I realized, because I felt Jacquie nudge my arm.

"Sorry, I thought she'd gotten some sort of fancy degree," I said.

"No idea. I never really interacted with her much," Jacquie answered. "Want to tell me why you insisted on a third wheel tonight?"

"I didn't," I began, but deflated moments later when she fixed me with a disbelieving look. "I just wasn't in the mood for a date night. To be honest, I'm not sure I'm really ready to be dating."

Jacquie jabbed a finger toward the bar. "Then tell him that, because in case it's escaped your notice, the man has fallen for you. Hard. And this team cannot work effectively if there is drama."

"It's not that I don't like him, it's just ... things are still kind of complicated with Kevin," I answered.

"You still see him around Headquarters?" she asked.

Kevin Ellery and I had begun our relationship while he was serving a sentence for murder. He had been manipulated and forced to do it by some very nasty people. He dumped me the day he'd been released. He'd insisted he needed to find himself without his magic, which on some level I could understand. We're supposed to keep magic hidden from the rest of the world and dealing with the loss of his while in prison wouldn't have been doable. However, it didn't mean I still didn't hurt seeing him at Authority Headquarters when our paths crossed.

"Kind of hard to avoid," I finally offered just as Duncan reappeared toting drinks.

"Molly said she's going to join us," he announced, producing a fourth glass as he inched closer to me to make room.

"I thought you were on a date," Jacquie quipped as Molly materialized beside her.

Molly offered up a single shouldered shrug. "He had to work. I get it. Besides, I thought we could all use a night out."

I sipped on the beer Duncan had ordered and

people watched as my colleagues talked around the table. I tuned out their words, my senses once again focusing on the other people around me. The couple at the end of the bar had finally left, but the magical groper was back, inching his way toward the dance floor again.

"Not today, asshole," I grumbled, setting my drink down on the table.

I was halfway across the space before anyone could stop me. I could see his target—a visibly drunk brunette swaying to the music even when the song had stopped.

"I thought I told you to get lost," I called.

"What? You gonna shoot me lady?" he laughed.

"Don't tempt me," I replied, stepping up closer and leaned in. I caught the nauseating odor of sweat and stale alcohol on his skin. "Trust me when I tell you if the owner catches you using magic in his bar, he'll ban you."

"I don't often agree with feds, but this one's got a point," Jonathan's baritone voice said from behind me.

Having spent enough time in his presence over the years, I was acutely aware of the power wafting off of him. He'd been born with a genetic defect that left him physically disfigured. He used magic to cover it up and present a handsome face on a hulking muscled body.

The groper swallowed, his Adam's apple bobbing noticeably in his throat before backpedaling for good this time. I watched him and his lackeys until they'd left the bar behind before turning to face Jonathan.

"I had that handled you know," I noted.

"My bar, my prerogative."

"You know, you could probably put some wards up to keep that from happening," I offered. "I know a girl who is great with magical security."

"I can handle my own security, *agent*," he replied, spitting out the last word like it was sour.

"You're dating one of us. I would have thought your aversion to law enforcement would have waned."

I watched him glance in Molly's direction before shaking his head. "Special circumstance. I still don't like cops in my bar."

"Then maybe you should stop letting us in," I muttered and returned to the table and my now lukewarm beer.

"You are off duty, remember," Duncan said, awkwardly stretching his left arm out like he wanted to wrap it around my shoulders before thinking better of it. Unfortunately, he'd committed to raising his arm so he pretended to stretch. It was a little cute, but mostly awkward as hell.

"Not when there are douchey frat boys trying to take advantage of vulnerable girls," I answered.

Jacquie opened her mouth to add her thoughts before stopping and slipping her hand into her pocket. She pulled out her phone, studied the screen, and pressed it to her ear, making a beeline for the exit of the club.

If it were possible, the ambience of the bar softened around us and the space looked less crowded as I finished my beer. Maybe it was the alcohol taking effect, but when I spotted Jacquie returning, I could swear she moved in slow motion. Her expression signaled something was off. I caught her lean over and whisper something to Molly before retracing her steps to the exit.

"Come on, outside," Molly said, gesturing for Duncan and me to follow.

The buzzed feeling dissipated as the sticky August evening air hit me. Jacquie was already halfway down the block when we finally caught up to her. When she spun to face us, I could see unshed tears making her eyes sparkle in the ambient light cast by the fluorescence in the nearby windows.

"What's going on?" Duncan asked.

"I just got a call from my niece," Jacquie replied.

Molly and I exchanged a knowing glance. Jacquie's niece, Neveah, could see the future. She'd been the one who'd foretold Ezri's death two years ago. Seeing the future was a heavy burden for a teenager to carry.

"What did she see?" I whispered.

"Her father's death."

TWO

I didn't know all of Jacquie's personal history, but I knew enough to be certain that her brother had died before our paths ever crossed. It was part of the reason Jacquie had taken temporary custody of Neveah and her older brother Troy while their mom got herself sorted out in rehab.

"You're telling me her powers are expanding?" Molly hissed.

"Okay, someone is going to need to fill me in," Duncan said.

Molly let out an exasperated huff, but said, "Jacquie's niece and nephew have magic. Neveah can see the future sometimes."

"Got it. So, she saw your brother's death. That's a good thing isn't it?" he replied.

"He died five years ago," Jacquie answered, her voice raw.

"Oh."

"Are you sure she saw your brother and not someone else? I mean, not that I'm a vision expert or anything. But aren't they usually kind of intentionally vague?" Molly nodded her agreement with my questions.

"All I know is that she told me she saw him die."

"Then what are we doing still standing here. We need to talk to her," I said. It wasn't quite a magical criminal case, but it was certainly a mystery.

"I drove. We can take my car," Molly announced and led us further down the block away from the bar to a small parking lot behind one of the other businesses.

We crammed into her car and she took off, ignoring several traffic lights in the process, on our way to Jacquie's sister-in-law's place. I tried to imagine what the experience of seeing her own father's death had been like for Neveah. She was a strong kid. She'd endured captivity at the hands of the Order of Samael two years ago and she was still a coherent, functional child. If I'd been in her place, I doubted I would have come through as well as she had.

Once we arrived, Jacquie was out of the passenger side of the car before Molly had even cut the engine. The front door to the house sat open and I could see Jacquie's nephew, Troy, standing there like he'd been expecting his aunt to burst in any minute with an FBI entourage.

"She's in her room, Aunt Jacquie," I heard Troy explain as I climbed out of the car.

"Did she tell you what she saw?" Jacquie demanded.

Troy shook his head. "I tried, but she insisted that she could only tell you. What is going on?"

Jacquie pulled the young man into an embrace. I could barely make out her lips moving as she whispered something to him. I hurried past Molly and Duncan, and stepped into the house just as Jacquie released her grip on the boy and headed upstairs. I followed suit, waiting just outside the bedroom door to give the girl some privacy with her aunt.

"You can come in," Jacquie called after a moment of silence.

I crossed the threshold into a room decked out in dark purples and pale pinks. I spotted posters on the walls for bands I hadn't even heard of. Still in pajamas Neveah sat in the middle of her bed, legs tucked under her as Jacquie perched on the edge, one hand resting on the girl's shoulder.

"Hi, Neveah, I don't know if you remember me," I said. "My name is Kayla."

"You knew Ezri," Neveah answered.

I nodded. "I did, yeah. Your aunt says you saw something pretty scary. How are you doing?"

"Confused," Neveah admitted. "I know it was my dad ... but that's not supposed to be possible since he's already dead. I can't see the past. At least, I've never seen it before."

"You've been spending a lot of time at headquarters lately," Jacquie noted. "Maybe all that practice is making your powers grow?"

"I don't want them to grow," Neveah answered, wrapping her arms around her aunt. "I don't want to see bad things like this anymore."

Had she seen more than just the vision that prophesied Ezri's sacrifice?

I made a mental note to ask Jacquie about it later when we were in private. "I know you don't want to see it again, but there's a reason you called Jacquie, right? You wanted her help?"

"Well, I can't talk to my mom about it. Anything about Dad just makes her upset. And she's been doing really good lately," Neveah answered.

"I'm sure Troy would have listened," Jacquie whispered.

"But he couldn't help," Neveah countered. "I don't know how to explain it, but it also felt like ... like a warning. It ended fast, but I thought I saw someone else. Someone I don't know and it felt like they were in danger."

I didn't want to make her relive what she'd seen. But if what she was saying was true and what she'd seen was some kind of warning of something else to come, then we needed as many details as possible. We needed someone with experience pulling memories out of people. Or at least studying them from within the memory.

"Damn it," I grumbled under my breath. It was loud enough for Jacquie to hear. "Sorry, I just ... it would have been really useful if Desmond was here."

"You're not wrong. But I think we might have another option," Jacquie answered.

Just then, footsteps sounded on the stairs followed by Duncan and Molly appearing in the doorway. "How can we help?" Molly's voice was soft and nonthreatening.

"We're going to need to make a trip. But I need to call Denise and let her know we're taking Neveah."

"I can let her know," Troy offered, squeezing between the two agents before moving to sit beside his sister on the bed.

"No, it should come from me," Jacquie answered with a shake of her head. She stood and eyed her niece. "Get dressed. We leave in five minutes."

Everyone, but Troy left the room, retreating to the first floor. He appeared a minute later and leaned against the front of the stove in the kitchen. "Can you please tell me what's going on? She hasn't been this freaked out since after the kidnapping," he looked directly at his aunt.

"She saw your father's death. She thinks it might be something like a warning," Jacquie replied.

"Wait. She sees the future, not the past," he noted.

"That's why we're going to get some professional help to understand exactly what she saw," Jacquie replied just as Neveah appeared in jean shorts and a t-shirt.

"Let's get in the car while Jacquie let's your mom know what's going on," I said, ushering the girl out to the car. It was a tight fit with the extra body, but Duncan and I managed to squeeze in without too much trouble.

"I'm sorry this keeps happening," I said as we

waited for Jacquie and Molly to join us. "It's not fair to you."

"Desmond used to say that we can't choose the gifts we're given and that even when something feels like a burden, it's there for a reason."

I smiled sadly at the mention of the man who'd pulled me out of a dark existence. "Sounds like him."

"I miss him," Neveah murmured.

Before I could share in her sentiment, Jacquie and Molly returned to the car. Troy stood in the doorway watching the car back out of the driveway. I turned my attention out the window as we moved through the sparse traffic on the roads. I wasn't sure where we were going, but I trusted Jacquie to know how to help her niece.

I still didn't recognize our surroundings when Jacquie eased the car to a stop outside an apartment complex. She climbed out and gestured for everyone else to follow suit. Moments later, we trailed behind her up to a closed door where she knocked briskly twice.

I could hear sounds coming from within the apartment. A part of me longed to turn invisible and walk right on in to see what was going on. But this was someone's home. Someone Jacquie trusted enough with her niece's secret and those instincts would only serve to get me in trouble.

Finally, after what felt like an interminable length of time, I heard the chain slide free of the lock and the door opened inward to reveal a familiar face. The tension that had crept into my body as we waited melted away at the sight of J.T. Somers. He was a paramedic and a magical healer.

"Jacquie, hey. I'm getting ready to head on shift," he said before peering out at our assembled group. "What's going on?"

"It's safer if we talk inside," Jacquie answered.

J.T. exhaled and nodded, his gaze settling on Neveah. "Sure."

He opened the door all the way and one by one we filed into the apartment I now realized he'd shared with Ezri. I spotted a couple of photos hanging on the living room wall from their wedding and my chest ached. He still clung to the woman he'd loved and lost.

"Neveah had a vision, but it was of something that's already happened," Jacquie explained. "I thought maybe you could help us see what she saw without making her relive it."

J.T. rubbed at his chin. "Memory magic was more Des' specialty. And Ezri's. But I can try." He looked at me. "Not to put you on the spot, but I could use a little magical boost if you're up for it."

"Yeah, of course."

"From experience, it's easier if you aren't toting too many onlookers," Molly volunteered. "I know we all want to know what Neveah saw. But seeing as you're doing us a favor, it's probably better we don't overwhelm you."

"I appreciate that," J.T. said. "Jacquie, why don't you come along?"

Her lips pressed into a thin line as she considered his request. I understood her apprehension. She needed to know what her niece had witnessed, but if it really depicted her brother's death, that wasn't something she needed to carry.

"Molly's done this before. She knows how it works. Why not her?" I suggested.

Jacquie's shoulders relaxed a fraction and she nodded. Molly gave Jacquie a reassuring pat on the shoulder and followed J.T. over to the couch where Neveah sat.

"You aren't going to feel anything, okay?" J.T. prepped the girl.

"I know. Desmond used to do it with me, Gabby, and Carly."

A wistful expression came over the medic, but it

passed moments later and he was all business. He held his hand out to me and I took it, clasping my other in Neveah's right hand. Molly took up a spot on Neveah's other side and I let my magic bubble to the surface.

Given how at the ready it had been at Notre Dame, it wasn't hard to get it to come out and play. Chamomile bloomed around me, coating my skin in a thick layer of magic.

No, I need to give him a signal boost.

I could almost feel my magic slithering across my skin, pooling in the small space between mine and J.T.'s palms. I could feel more than smell his magic. It was like a protective bubble had enveloped us.

"Okay, Neveah, I need you to think about what you saw, bring it to the front of your thoughts so we can see it, too," J.T. coached.

"Okay." Neveah's voice was soft as she sunk deeper into the couch.

Slowly, the living room around us melted away and we were in the back seat of a car. The sky was dark beyond the windshield as a man with thick dark curls sat behind the wheel. I'd never met the man, but I had no reason to doubt this was Jacquie's brother. The scene unfolded in front of us at normal speed and the driver craned his neck trying to peer out the rear window. I pivoted to follow his gaze, but saw nothing out of the ordinary.

"You thought you could get out?" an ethereal male voice called, filling the car.

"This isn't real," Jacquie's brother said, shaking his head. "You're not really here."

The voice laughed and it made my teeth ache. "Oh, I am very much here, Jamal. But you won't be for long."

Jamal's body jerked and his hands tightened on the wheel, spinning it sharply to the left toward oncoming traffic. He managed to fix his gaze on the rearview mirror and from my position I could see the fear in his expression. Whatever was in this car with him had taken control of his body and wasn't letting go.

"No one gets free," the voice taunted just as the car spun, slammed through the guardrail, and into another car. The image shifted just as Neveah had suggested and I caught a glimpse of a woman I didn't recognize sitting behind the wheel of another car. But that same shadowy figure consumed her. A look of fear filled her eyes just before a tractor trailer came into view.

The image paused mid-motion and I breathed a sigh of relief we wouldn't have to see the car go up in flames. I could feel J.T.'s magic trying to keep the spell going.

"I need a different angle," I muttered and let out a little more of my own power.

The scene rewound past the woman, bringing Jamal into the picture and we were back in his car. It remained stationary, that look of fear frozen on Jamal's face. I moved around the space, ignoring the laws of physics as I went. I now stood outside the vehicle and had a clear view inside. I could make out something shadowy in the car, almost like mist or fog. But it had no real form. What the hell?

The vision faded, replaced again by J.T.'s living room. I let go of Neveah's hand and stood to face Jacquie. "Before I tell you what we saw, I need to know what you do about your brother's death?"

"He was killed in a car accident. The medical examiner said he had a seizure and lost control of the wheel."

"Did he have a history of seizures or epilepsy?"

Jacquie shook her head. "No. I thought something about it didn't make sense, but Denise begged me to let it go. I knew she was in pain and I knew the kids didn't need me obsessing, so I let it go." Color drained from her cheeks. "What happened to my brother, Kayla?"

"There was something in the car with him. I couldn't see it exactly, but whatever it was spoke to him and it took over his body. It forced him to drive into traffic. He didn't have a seizure. Magic killed your brother."

"What about the warning?" Duncan interjected.

"I don't know. It said, 'No one gets free,' right before it killed Jamal. That seemed pretty foreboding. And it kept taunting him about thinking he'd gotten out. But I also caught a glimpse of a woman, suffering the same fate as Jamal. I think we're supposed to find her ... and save her." I answered, turning to look at Neveah curled up on the couch. J.T. had gone into the kitchen and come back out with a glass of water.

"I was pretty focused on my own career back then. I'd just made Detective and I wanted to make a good impression. I didn't need to be seen cleaning up my brother's messes," Jacque said, sounding ashamed. "I tried not to pay too much attention to what he did with his time."

"He was away a lot before it happened," Neveah offered. "I remember he would go away for a couple days at a time. But he'd always come back and he'd have little gifts for Troy and me. I think Dad thought we didn't notice."

"That's good, Neveah. That's really good," I said, trying to catalog the information in my mind. There was a reason this was all coming up now and we were going to find out what it was.

"Jacquie, could your reluctance to look into this be related to his death somehow?" Molly wondered. "If magic was used to kill him, maybe it was used to nudge you away from following your cop instincts."

"Maybe. But there's nothing stopping me from digging now." She waved for Neveah to stand up. "Let's get you home."

"You just had to taunt the universe about not getting a magical case, didn't you?" Duncan whispered in my ear as we left J.T. in his living room.

"If it helps Jacquie, I'll taunt the universe all day long," I retorted, then turned to Jacquie and asked, "So, where are we going next, boss?"

"Back to the office. I need to call in a favor."

Jacquie disappeared into her office as soon as we'd dropped Neveah off at home and gotten back to FBI headquarters. I could hear her pacing back and forth, her voice low. Duncan and Molly disappeared into the conference room and by the squeaking sound of dry erase marker on white board, they were starting to assemble what we knew.

I joined them in the conference room to find Molly capping the marker. The information scrawled across the pale surface wasn't much—Jamal's name and some details that she'd picked up on from viewing Neveah's vision. She'd also noted 'shadow creature' with a question mark at the end.

"Any idea why all of this would be coming up now?" Duncan asked.

"No clue, but there are clearly pieces to this puzzle that we're missing," I said, moving to stand beside my colleagues. "Where was he headed that night? If magic was used to kill him, who was behind it? And why?"

"I don't have any of those answers, but someone should be coming by with my brother's case file," Jacquie said, filling the doorway. "Captain Beech owed me a favor," she added, looking to Molly.

"You don't remember anything from that period? About what might have been going on in his life?" Molly pressed.

"Like I said, I was focused on my job. I blocked him out."

"We're going to figure this out," I told her.

"There's got to be more we could have gotten from seeing Neveah's vision," Jacquie said.

"We were in and out to avoid putting too much strain on Neveah," I noted.

"She's not wrong, though," Molly stated. "There's probably more that the two of us missed."

There was no way we were going to put a teenage girl through witnessing her father's murder a third time. An idea took root in the back of my mind. I hated it already, but it was the only option I could think of.

"So, I might have a way," I said after taking a steadying breath. "I could try and project it from my memory for the three of you to see."

"Have you done that before?" Duncan asked, his voice hushed.

"Nope. No idea if it will actually work, but magic can do a lot of things most people would call impossible."

"What sort of strain would that take?" Molly probed.

"She's stronger than you think," Jacquie intervened before I could respond.

I wasn't sure I believed in her vote of confidence. However, I didn't feel I was in a position to argue with the woman who'd just learned her brother's death had been orchestrated at the hands of someone magical.

"I can handle it," I finally said.

"What do you need?" Molly looked resigned to the fact we were doing this.

"Space," I replied.

Jacquie and Duncan moved toward the chairs and long conference table, but I blocked their path. It would take too long to move them manually and it felt like we were operating against a clock whose time we couldn't see yet. Chamomile cascaded over my skin and the chairs and table vanished. I envisioned them rematerializing in the cubicle space beyond the conference room.

"Damn." Duncan's comment signaled it had been successful.

"Give me some space," I said, stepping into the middle of the now empty conference room.

I closed my eyes and concentrated. Not on the scene in J.T.'s living room, but in what Neveah had showed us from her vision. I could feel her pain and fear like an undercurrent as I pulled the image from my own mind.

Come on, Kayla. Focus.

I blocked out the emotions and concentrated on the details—the space of the car, the direction it had traveled, Jamal behind the wheel. When it solidified in my mind's eye, I let out more power, with the simple thought: *let them see.*

Heat washed over me, churning my stomach, but I stood still until the feeling subsided. I opened my eyes to find we no longer stood in the conference room, but in an enlarged version of the interior of Jamal's car.

"Okay, I don't know how long I'm going to be able to sustain this. So, work fast," I said.

I watched as Duncan took a few steps back, so he

was even with where I stood. He faced the front of the vehicle and his brow knit together. Only I was too focused on keeping the spell going, I couldn't pay attention to whatever he saw.

"He had GPS on," he announced helpfully.

Molly stepped in front of me, blocking my view. "He was headed here."

That was enough to break my concentration and I took a step forward. "What?"

She moved aside so I could have full access to the car's navigation system. Sure, enough the address displayed at the top of the screen was the building in which we now stood.

"Jacquie, would Jamal have had any reason to be going to the FBI?"

"We aren't the only agency in this building," Duncan pointed out.

"Somehow, I doubt he was going to file a complaint about his job," I noted.

"To answer your question, no I don't know if he would have reason to come here," Jacquie answered with a frustrated sigh.

"Not to be pushy, but can we keep this moving?" I asked, sweat popping out along my hairline as I did my best to keep the spell going.

Molly knelt down in what would have been the

front passenger seat, studying something that had slid beneath the seat. "It looks like there's a document under there." She grasped for it, but her fingers came up empty. "Memory, right," she muttered more to herself than the rest of us.

"Can you tell anything about the thing that overtook him?" Jacquie's question was clearly directed my way.

I pivoted to face the back of the room and the image of the back seat. I could see something dark and smoke-like filling the space, but this was a vision from a child who hadn't been there. It wasn't really a memory I could relive. The magic that had been present in the car years ago would be long-gone by now. Still, I thought I could make out the edges of something humanoid. I glanced over to Jacquie.

"Did they find anything else in the car besides Jamal's DNA?"

Before she could answer, her phone rang. She snatched it from her pocket. "Agent DeWitt." A pause and then "Send them up." For a moment I wondered who had called her. Our usual security left at five o'clock. Then again, I hadn't had a reason to be in the building this late before.

She paused long enough to draw the blinds in the interior window and ease the door shut before stepping into the cubicle area. I heard her grumbling under her breath as she navigated around the relocated furniture.

"You didn't have to bring it over yourself," I heard Jacquie tell whoever had just entered the office.

"It's me, Jacquie. You call and ask for something like this, I know how personal it is. I'm not trusting t with anyone else," a female voice responded.

I peered through the closed blinds to see Jacquie accept a slim case file from another woman. I didn't recognize her, but the way she looked at Jacquie told me they had history.

"Uh, Kayla," Molly's voice drew me back to the room and I turned in time to see the interior of the car flicker out of existence.

"Shit, sorry," I muttered and balled my hands into fists. My magic pulsed against my fingers as I poured it back into the spell.

"You were asking about any other DNA in the car," Duncan said, redirecting the focus back to what I'd noticed. "Why?"

"I can sort of make out a person, at least the outline of one, under all this smoke. That suggests they were actually in the car with Jamal."

"Instead, of what, remotely taking control?" he replied.

"Yes. Most magic is better when there's a physical connection. But I would guess our killer knew what the outcome was going to be and would need an exit strategy."

The conference room door opened and Jacquie stepped back in, the police file falling open against her palms. "No traces of any foreign DNA."

"Then our killer had a magical exit strategy," I noted.

"They were hidden from him, right?" Duncan began to pace the width of the room. "Could we be dealing with more, uh, Whisperers?"

"Unfortunately, invisibility isn't unique to just us. Any practitioner has the ability to do it. And if we were dealing with a Whisperer, they wouldn't have need of the smoke to obscure their identity."

"You're sure about that?" Jacquie sounded skeptical.

I was going to have one hell of a magical hangover in the morning, but it was easier to prove my point with magic. I loosened my hold on the power within me, letting it seep back into me, hiding me away.

Just enough so they can't see me.

I watched my colleagues' faces as I vanished. "I can still talk to you even if you can't see me," I said before returning to a corporeal state. "No creepy smoke needed."

Unfortunately, my body chose that moment to reach its limit and the car interior vanished around us. My head throbbed and I staggered sideways into the blinds. Of course, I'd moved all the damn chairs out of the room. I slid down to the floor and sucked in gulps of air.

"I think maybe we all need a few hours of sleep," Molly decreed.

"No, I'll be okay," I said even as my surroundings greyed out at the edges. "I just need a minute ... to ... catch my breath."

"No. You need sleep. We all do," she argued.

"We could be wasting time," Jacquie protested. "We still don't know why Neveah saw this now. And she insisted it felt like a warning. Lives could be at risk."

I suspected she also wanted to comb through the file on Jamal's death. If nothing else, to assuage her guilt about not doing so years ago. Molly shook her head, standing firm.

"Believe me, I understand how important this is to you, Jacquie. And that is why if we are going to figure this out, we are all going to need to be at our best. That means everyone goes home and I don't want to see you back here before seven. That's an order."

I nodded as much as my throbbing head would allow and squeezed my eyes shut to ward off the nausea. I heard fabric rustle and felt Duncan's hand cup my right shoulder.

"I'll drive you home," he offered.

"Thanks."

We sat there for a few minutes until I'd regained command of my senses enough to stand and follow him downstairs. As we drove to my apartment, I tried to process everything we'd come across so far. It was a five-year-old case where most of the physical evidence was likely no longer available and there was magic involved that I couldn't identify.

I was also certain that any sleep I got tonight would be plagued by images of Jamal's death. I could still hear that creepy fucking voice taunting the poor guy. And when I closed my eyes, I saw Jamal's fear frozen in his expression within the rearview mirror as he realized he wasn't going to see his kids or wife again. That whatever he'd been mixed up in was going to get him killed.

I was grateful, at least, that Jacquie wouldn't

have to carry that burden, too. But Neveah would. I fought to hold back hot tears at that thought. She was just a child, an innocent child. The poor girl had endured so much in the last few years simply because of the power she'd been born with. I honestly didn't know how she managed not to lose her mind in the process. Magic was a real bitch sometimes.

"We're going to figure this out," Duncan said as he eased the car to a stop outside my apartment building. "I didn't say it before, but what you did back there was really impressive."

I offered a weak wave, as if to say, 'yay me.' "Sometimes I forget that this isn't supposed to come easy to me. I've seen people with so much more power just throw it around like it was nothing and I have to keep reminding myself that I'm not them. I wanted to help Jacquie and I pushed myself."

"Will rest help?'

"Mostly. And time away from doing magic, too." Too bad my gut told me that we were going to need my magic and sooner than I was comfortable with.

"Well, at least you can go and rest. We'll start fresh in the morning," he replied.

"There are just so many unanswered questions.

How the hell are we supposed to investigate something when the evidence is long gone?"

He flashed me a mischievous smile. Normally, I would find that boyish excitement amusing, sexy even, but right now I was just too worn out to tolerate it. "What?"

"I might have an idea or two on how to handle that. Or rather, I might know a guy who knows a guy who might be able to do me a favor to find out if my hunch is right."

That sounded an awful lot like he was planning an all-nighter. And as much as I knew he was a grown man who could make his own shitty decisions, I didn't want to see him get chewed out tomorrow. "If you show up tomorrow morning looking like you haven't slept, Molly is going to have your ass."

"Then we're all very lucky I can operate on very little sleep. I've got this. You did your part, let me do mine." He leaned over and pecked me on the cheek before I climbed out of the car and dragged my weary body inside.

I made a beeline for the bathroom where I rummaged through the medicine cabinet, looking for anything that might help abate the pounding in my temples and keep the nightmares at bay. I found a glass container with a handwritten label for sleeping tablets. I tipped one out into my palm and the scent of honey washed over me. Just like at J.T.'s place.

I had forgotten he'd given them to me. "Bottoms up." Time to see if his healing magic was as good as everyone said.

AUGUST 10, 2019

FOUR

J.T. was a fucking miracle worker. The next morning, I woke up feeling more refreshed than I had in months. Probably since before I graduated from Quantico. And even better, Jamal's death hadn't plagued me in the least. I made a mental note to suggest that Jacquie talk to J.T. about getting some of those pills for Neveah.

It was no surprise that I wasn't the first in the office just shy of seven o'clock. At least everyone was wearing new clothes and actually looked like they'd taken Molly's orders to heart. Duncan paced in the corner of the conference room; cell phone pressed to his ear. Someone had moved the table and chairs back into the room and Jacquie sat flipping through the pages of the police file.

"Finding anything that might help?" I asked, pulling the chair out beside her with more force than necessary to ensure it made noise.

She looked up at me. "The accident report confirms that he went through the guard rail into oncoming traffic. They tested him for drugs and alcohol, but he was clean."

"Which is what led them to think seizure?" I replied.

"The report didn't say it specifically. The cause of death was injuries sustained in the accident."

"Mitch, come on, you owe me one," Duncan said, his voice interrupting our conversation.

"He's been calling around to the junk yards."

Maybe this Mitch guy was the one who owed him a favor. "He thinks the car might be impounded somewhere even all this time later?"

"I know we're grasping at straws, but it's worth a shot," Jacquie replied.

"Thank you for seeing it my way," Duncan said and ended the call. When he turned to face us, he wore a broad grin. "I think we might actually be in luck. My cousin Mitch owns an impound lot. He owes me for hosting Thanksgiving for the last two years," he explained.

Jacquie and I exchanged incredulous looks

before he continued. "If you know our family, you know it's a big deal. Anyway, he usually doesn't give out that kind of information, but I told him if he did me this favor, I'd host the next two years."

"You mean to tell me he keeps track of every car that comes into his lot?" I blurted.

"Mitch is very meticulous. I gave him the plate number, the VIN, and he had it in his records. He said we could come out and take a look today."

"Are you sure he's not screwing with you just to get out of Thanksgiving hosting duties?" I retorted. "I mean, what are the odds he has a car from five years ago. What, does he not compact anything?"

"Like I said, Mitch is meticulous."

"You two go check out the car. I'm going to stay here and try to keep digging into what I can from the police records," Jacquie said.

That wasn't the reaction I'd expected from her. I'd have thought she'd be pushing us out of her way to get to the car. It was then that I realized Molly was MIA. I doubted she would have given us the directive to stay away until now only to sleep in.

"Where's Molly?" I stayed seated.

"She went down to the coroner's office to see if there was anything else she could glean from them.

I'd have gone except the one Medical Examiner I'm on good terms with didn't work the case."

I was still getting used to the idea that we had certain people we expected to work with. Duncan waited by the door, car keys in hand. "Can I borrow this for one second?" I pointed to the file sitting in front of Jacquie.

She slid it across the table to me and I flipped through it quickly, locating the information we needed—make, model and other identifying information of Jamal's car. I snapped a picture with my phone before following Duncan out of the office.

"How'd you sleep?" he asked once we were on the road.

"Good. I'm not sure I'd be up for slinging a ton of magic around, but better than yesterday."

"Do I want to know how you managed that?" He gave me a skeptical eyebrow raise. "When I dropped you off, you looked pretty rough."

"Would you believe me if I said magic pills?"

"Given everything we've been through, yeah I would.

I grinned. "Magic pills. But don't worry, they were prescribed by a healer."

"Your paramedic friend."

"I wouldn't call him a friend exactly. More of an

acquaintance. We know the same people in the magical community. But he's a good guy and we can trust him."

"Well, whatever helped, I'm glad it worked. I was worried about you for a minute," he said as we pulled up to a metal gate.

I could see rows and rows of cars stacked high. I sat there, studying the rows and rows of banged up vehicles. Until it hit me, they were all color coded. "Uh, you weren't kidding when you said Mitch was meticulous," I murmured.

Duncan let out a laugh. "He's got OCD and sometimes, it's a blessing."

"Like trying to find a five-year-old busted up car," I muttered and waited as the gates swung inward, allowing us entrance.

I still couldn't shake the feeling this was going to be a wasted trip. What were the odds that the exact car we were looking for just happened to have ended up in his cousin's lot? I knew the universe sometimes had a funny way of doling out fate, but this appeared even beyond what could be plausible. A stout man with a thick neck and beefy biceps stepped out of a guard booth and approached us. I paused, hand hovering near my holster for a moment until he pulled Duncan into a hug.

"You are doing me a real solid," Mitch said, releasing my partner.

His enthusiasm didn't quite fit with Duncan's demeanor while on the phone with him. After a moment, Duncan pushed his cousin away and cleared his throat. "I appreciate you opening up early to let us have a look at the car."

"Sure, sure," Mitch answered and disappeared into the guard booth.

I stepped up beside Duncan and whispered, "You could have just told him it was part of an ongoing criminal investigation and that should have been enough to get him to cooperate."

"Believe me, if it were that easy I would have. Asking Mitch to disrupt his patterns is a big deal. Like I said, he's got OCD and that means he's got a very particular way of doing things."

"Got it!" Mitch called and reappeared before leading us through the neatly ordered rows of cars.

As I passed, I noticed that every row had the same number of cars stacked, even if the heights varied. We moved between towering heaps of Priuses and Toyotas, past a row of silver Lexuses, and finally to a row of dark red vehicles. I tried to read the mangled license plates. Though even with consulting my phone for the information I'd taken from the case file, I still didn't see what we were looking for.

"You're sure it's here?" I said, annoyance coloring my tone. "Because if you're screwing with us I could arrest you for obstructing a federal investigation."

"Whoa! There's no need for that," Mitch said and gestured high above us. "The one you're looking for is up there. You're lucky you called when you did. I was actually getting ready to crush the top half of this pile."

"Why?" I couldn't help asking the question.

"Because I do them by the year they came in and then by color."

Duncan mouthed 'I told you so' as Mitch puttered around, climbing into a machine with a large grabber attachment. He fired it up, the engine rumbling loudly in my ears as it reached up and plucked the vehicle off the pile like he was playing a carnival game. I winced as metal crunched and whined under the pressure of the grabber.

"Take it easy!" I yelled over the machinery whirring.

He couldn't hear me. Once he'd freed it from the pile, he navigated through the stacks to a larger, more open space and set the car down on the ground. My heart hammered in my ears as I approached the car. It had seen better days. Both the front and rear bumpers had been sheered clean off the car. The trunk had collapsed and the hood sat partially crumpled, too.

"This is going to be tricky," I told Duncan. I tugged on the passenger side door and it stuck. "Help me."

He squeezed beside me and together we yanked on the handle. After a few good tugs, the latch gave way and the door creaked on weakened hinges.

"It was under the seat," Duncan noted, intentionally vague in his cousin's presence.

I knelt down, my right hand groping beneath the front seat, hoping to find the file Molly had spotted in the vision. I couldn't feel anything, but that didn't mean much. It could have been thrown into the back seat or wedged against something else.

"Let's see if we can get in the back," I said.

Duncan arched a brow. "Even if we could get the door open, neither of us is going to be able to fit in there."

"Not strictly true," I reminded him.

"You shouldn't push yourself."

"It would only take a minute or two. I can handle

that much," I said, brushing off his concern. "Just distract Mitch."

"I think you've got the easier job," he snickered, but disappeared from view.

He was right about one thing; it was going to be a tight fit, even with magic. But I didn't need to get the rear door open to get in. I crawled into the front seat and sat there in the musty space for a moment and I couldn't help picturing Jamal in the driver seat next to me. Had he reached for the file beneath the passenger seat to try and keep it out of view? Peering over the headrest into the back of the car, I thought I saw something resembling paper peeking out from under the floor mats.

I was no physics expert. Yet I supposed it was possible with the car spinning and crashing, all of the momentum could have forced the file to slip beneath something else.

Time to go digging the magical way.

As I'd done yesterday, I let my magic wash over me. I had finally found a balance with the power inside of me, where I wasn't afraid it would turn on me of its own accord. Even still, there were times I was still hesitant to let it hide me away from the world. Some habits were too easy to fall back into. I'd managed to not let my past drag me back down a few months ago, but it hadn't been easy.

I had to constantly remind myself that I was in control of the magic, not the other way around. It had to obey me, not the other way around.

"Focus, Kayla. Come on. Jacquie is counting on you," I said, hoping the pep talk would steady my nerves.

I just needed to become incorporeal long enough to slip into the back seat and look around. That should be easy. I'd passed through plenty of walls and barriers thicker than the seat of a car. Slowly, my hands and forearms vanished. I felt the magic creep up my body until all of me had disappeared. It always still amazed me how I retained body aware-ness even when I couldn't see it. One of the many things Lola had taught me. A pang of guilt tightened my chest at the thought of the woman who'd given me a place in the world after my magic turned on me. Luckily, I'd gotten out of that life. She'd been sucked in so deep and it had cost her everything. Time to put her lessons to good use for once.

Pressing my hands against the back of the passenger seat, I moved through the thick faux leather fabric and tipped down, landing on the floor in the cramped space between the backseat and the front. I let out a little grunt at the sudden change in orientation. The trunk's collapse had limited the space back here even more.

As I did my best to twist around in the small space, I noticed something indented in the faux leather material of the back seat. It almost looked like the indent someone would leave behind after sitting in the car for a long time. Someone with a lot of weight.

It was illogical and irrational, but for a moment, I pictured Mitch sitting in the vehicle. He was hefty enough to leave a mark like that, even all these years later. And if he'd been running the lot five years ago, it would have been easy for him to secure the contract to take the car.

No, it was just my brain trying to make connections anywhere it could. I pushed the image of the indent aside and went on with my file search. I dug my nails into the scratchy floor mats pinned behind the driver seat and peeled them back. Dirty floor and bits of shattered glass clung to the underside of the mat, but no documents revealed themselves.

"You know, you never told me why you do it by year *and* color," Duncan's voice was too loud. Too close.

I blocked out Mitch's reply as I turned to the mat

beneath my knees. Just because I was currently invisible didn't mean I still didn't have mass. Unless I was moving through solid structures, if I wasn't paying attention, people could bump into me in this state. I eased onto the back seat and braced my feet as best I could against the center console to my left with the doorframe on my right. I yanked the mat up to reveal a dusty, slightly wrinkled manila file.

Well, damn. Maybe the universe is on our side after all.

I scooped it up, tucking it close to my body. Focusing I moved back through the front seat and emerged, letting the magic hiding me drop away as I did so. I caught Duncan's gaze and nodded.

"Thanks again for the help, Mitch. See you for Thanksgiving," he said to his cousin, clapping him on the shoulder.

I followed my partner through the rows of stacked cars and back to where we'd parked at the front of the lot. I held up the file once we were in the safety of his car.

"It ended up under the floor mat," I explained, then adding, "I hope whatever is in here points us to who wanted Jamal dead."

Before Duncan could respond, his phone rang, flashing Molly's number on the screen. He tapped the 'Accept' button and set the call to speakerphone. "Hey boss."

"You two on your way back yet?"

"Just about to leave. Why, what's going on?"

"I think we might have figured out why Jamal was headed to the FBI."

FIVE

Thanks to Duncan's erratic driving back to the office at top speed, I didn't have a chance to review the file we'd found in Jamal's car. Molly's words played over and over in my head: *I think we might have figured out why Jamal was headed to the FBI.*

Had they found something in the file Jacquie had gotten from the police? Had Neveah seen something else that had provided a clue? Despite my irritation at not being able to review the file in my lap, I silently urged Duncan to go even faster to reach our destination.

"What did you find?" I blurted the moment we were finally in the conference room.

Jacquie turned from her position at the whiteboard to respond, her gaze traveling to the file in my hand. "Looks like we've both got some news to share."

"Honestly, we haven't had a chance to go through it. But what did you find?" I repeated.

"I had a hunch," Molly began, turning a laptop so the screen faced away from her. "You were probably right that he was coming here that night to see someone in the FBI offices. So, I ran his name through the database and it returned a single hit."

"He was involved in a case?" Duncan sounded surprised.

"Admittedly, I'm not sure because the file is restricted," she replied. "But from what I can gather he's noted as a person of interest and a potential witness."

"Well, you've got higher security clearance than all of us. Can't you get access?" I demanded.

Molly shook her head. "Believe me, I tried. Got booted out of the system twice. I wasn't going to make it three strikes."

"So, how do you know why he was coming here if you don't know what case he might have been involved in?"

"Because his cell phone was logged into evidence after the crash. Denise never bothered to pick it up and it got shelved when the case file moved to storage," Jacquie answered.

I watched as she produced a clear evidence bag with a cell phone nestled inside. Given it had been five years, I doubted it had any battery remaining. And if by some miracle it did, there was no guarantee we'd be able to gain access to it.

"So, we've got an electronic case file we can't access and a phone that's probably dead and password protected," I sighed and looked at my colleagues. The slight downturn of Molly's lips, coupled with her own sigh suggested we were having the same thought.

"Something tells me we don't have the time to go through all the proper channels," Duncan said.

"We could ask Avery," I offered.

"She's got her own life to live. We can't keep relying on her," Molly answered dismissively.

"She's helped us before and come on, she loves this kind of stuff," I offered.

"If she gets caught—" Molly began.

"She'll be covering her tracks with magic. I think she'll be fine," Jacquie interjected. "We need to know what is in that file and what might be hiding on his phone."

"Not to mention that woman I saw at the end of Neveah's vision. The one who is in danger."

I'd almost forgotten about her in my bid to be the one person everyone relied on when it came to magic. It had been just a glimpse, but I knew she was still there, stored in my memory somewhere. I just had to access her. Not to mention, the folder we'd recovered from Jamal's junked car.

"We did manage to find this," I said, holding up the folder.

"We didn't get a chance to look through it before you called," Duncan explained.

"Well, there's no time like the present," Molly nudged.

I settled at the conference table and eased the folder open. The first few pages were printed pictures, likely taken with a smart phone, of ledgers and bank transactions. Some looked to be taken of computer screens, while others were clearly kept on paper. The handwriting on the paper ledgers was cramped, nearly unreadable except for the dates and dollar amounts. Most of them ranged high in five figures. The later pages contained photos of squalid conditions with evidence of blood and other stains marring the floor. I spotted chains on one wall.

What the hell was he involved in?

The last page was a list of shipping companies and other information I didn't quite understand. I was beginning to appreciate why the case file was so restricted. Whatever was going on here was seriously fucked up.

"Jacquie, Neveah said that Jamal would be away for a couple days at a time. Did he have this phone for a long time?" I gestured to the bricked device sitting on the table.

"I don't know. Why?"

"If we could get it up and running, if he used a car to get wherever he was going, we'd be able to pinpoint what he was up to."

"Then I guess we'd better go pay Avery a visit after all," Molly replied.

"You go on ahead, I need to talk to Neveah and Troy," Jacquie said. When I gave her a quizzical look, she added, "If they can remember when he went away and came back, or what he brought them, it might help us narrow down the data we're looking for."

It made sense. But in some small way it also felt like she was avoiding the reality that her brother was involved in something dark and nefarious. Not that I could blame her. Finding out the people we love are capable of such evil things is never easy.

"Why don't I go with you?" Duncan offered, standing up and gesturing for Jacquie to lead the way.

Her jaw worked like she wanted to say something in response, but she stayed silent. That left Molly and I in the conference room. She scooped up the police file, along with the folder we'd recovered from the impound lot and marched toward the door.

"You really don't think Avery will help?" I asked as we made our way to her car.

"It's not that. I know she's a formal consultant now, but I feel kind of guilty asking her to magically force things for us."

"But that's why we have magic. To help us do things," I reminded her.

"You know, we were perfectly capable of doing our jobs before we knew magic existed," she muttered.

"Okay, what's going on? You are one of the most magic-friendly people I know. Why are you suddenly so down on the idea?" I said, looking at her apprehensively.

"I don't know," she admitted and slid behind the wheel. "It just feels like every time magic is involved, the people I care about are prone to get hurt and I'm tired of it."

"I just overdid it a little last night. I'm totally fine now," I said.

"It's not just you and this case. Or even the last one."

"You mean Ezri," I whispered.

"I saw the good she did, the people she helped, and it just seems like a waste that she was only here for such a short time."

"That's the thing about the Savior, you don't get to choose. But the rest of us, we can decide how we use the power we've been given. And I'm choosing to use it to help a friend find out the truth about her brother's death, and maybe save someone else's life in the process."

Molly looked at me. "Thanks for the pep talk. Maybe I didn't follow my own advice and get some sleep last night."

"We're going to figure out what happened to Jamal and stop it from happening to anyone else," I said, as much to convince my friend as to make myself believe the words.

The rest of the drive to Authority Headquarters was quiet. There weren't many cars on the road going out of the city, so we made excellent time, pulling into the circular driveway twenty minutes later.

"Are we sure she's going to be in?" Molly asked the question just as it came into my own head.

"Guess we'll find out," I answered and climbed out of the passenger seat.

We were halfway to the front steps when the doors swung inward and a gangly preteen boy appeared. He looked at us sheepishly when he saw he wasn't alone. I stopped in my tracks. The teenager momentarily morphing into the little boy I'd first met when Lola had first pulled me under her wing—her little brother Teddy. I knew he'd been coming around headquarters in the years since his sister's death, but I somehow hadn't realized he'd gotten this big so fast.

"Hi Teddy," I said, my throat going dry.

"Uh, hi," he answered, looking at me in confusion.

"We're looking for Avery Fellowes. You don't happen to know if she's around do you?" I posed, deciding he didn't need me to dredge up the memory of his sister.

He glanced over his shoulder before turning back to face us. "She's been staying here late a lot. Like, a lot."

That answered our question.

"Thanks." I took the steps two at a time, reaching

where he stood in a matter of seconds. "You have someone to get you home?"

He held out a phone with a ride share app pulled up. He definitely wasn't old enough to be using one of those without a guardian's consent. "I'm good. Thanks." He paused for a moment, looking at me with a narrowed gaze. "Have we met?"

"A long time ago. It's good to see you, Teddy," I said and stepped into the foyer.

Molly followed after me as I led the way to the second-floor meeting room that linked up with the tech hub. True to Teddy's word, Avery sat at her desk surrounded by monitors and whirring desktop towers.

"Sorry to interrupt," I said, knocking on the door-frame to announce our presence.

Avery spun to face us and I could see the dark circles under her eyes, barely hidden by the rims of her glasses. "Jacquie texted you were coming."

"Did she also tell you what's going on?" I leaned against a free stretch of desk.

"No. But I got a call this morning from J.T. warning me I might be getting a visit. He said something about Jacquie's niece having a weird vision."

"Of her father's death," Molly explained.

"His murder," I corrected. "I'm pretty sure something magical killed him. And there was a glimpse of a woman we think might be next on the killer's hit list."

"And you want me to do what exactly?"

"See if you can get into Jamal's phone," I said, holding up the evidence bag.

"And maybe hack a secure FBI case file," Molly added.

Avery stared at us and after an uncomfortable moment of silence asked, "Is that all? A little light crime?"

"It's for a good cause," I suggested. "And it would help Jacquie and her family put this to rest. Please."

She pulled off her glasses and rubbed the bridge of her nose. "Of course, I'm going to help." She pointed to the evidence bag. "I know I'm literally magic, but even I can't bring a dead cell battery back to life. I've got chargers over there. Plug it in. I can't do anything with it until it's charged."

Out of an abundance of caution, I donned latex gloves before sliding the phone out of the bag and hooking it into a corresponding charger. Jamal must have had the phone set to vibrate, because I could swear I felt a little jolt as power started to flow.

"I've already got some access to FBI case databases for the occasional consultation with both the locals and feds," Every continued. "I'm going to need whatever information you've got though."

Molly handed over the information Avery needed and I stood back to watch the woman work. I could feel, more than see, her magic as it bubbled up around her. I thought I caught the computer screen ripple for a moment as she continued to work, manipulating the technology before her.

Maybe because I'd never been present when Avery literally worked her magic on tech, I had a poor sense of how long something like this should take. Her fingers flew over the keyboard, while the mouse dipped in and out of view on the screen. At one point, she glanced over her shoulder at Molly and me.

"You might want to go get coffee or something. It's going to take a while. This is seriously encrypted. Like, I've never seen stuff this protected from other people within the same agency."

That made my stomach do an uncomfortable flip. "That can't be good."

Molly pulled her phone out of her pocket and eyed the screen. "We should check in with Jacquie and Duncan anyway. See what they've found."

I wanted to protest that there hadn't been enough time for them to have jogged the kids' memories, but knew it would be futile. Molly was my superior, no matter how friendly we were with each other, and that meant I had to follow her lead.

"Let us know the minute you get in," Molly directed at Avery.

Avery offered a brief thumb's up, but gave no verbal response.

Molly and I moved into the Council Chamber room and I took in the space. I'd only ever passed through here on my way to see Avery. I wasn't part of the council and that meant I didn't have a reason to be in this space.

Some people might find it elitist and archaic to have a governing body like this, but I didn't mind it. The people on the council changed over time, bringing in fresh ideas and perspectives. Besides, someone needed to set and carry out the rules, otherwise we would all fall into chaos and anarchy. Magic without a purpose was dangerous.

"What do you think Jamal was mixed up in?" I posed, the empty room bouncing my voice around the space.

"If someone had used magic to kill him and make it look like an accident, nothing good. What I don't get is if his name was linked to an FBI case, why didn't they go looking for the car?"

"Maybe they didn't know he had anything with him? Or they didn't know he was coming?" I offered. "I mean, the car was pretty mangled and the folder, with whatever that evidence was, had slid under a floor mat. I was lucky to have found it."

"And why protect a case file so heavily?" she grumbled.

"Uh, you guys still here?" Avery's voice floated out to us from the tech hub.

Molly and I exchanged a surprised look before rushing back into the room to find Avery staring at an electronic case file with two words in the heading I'd never expected to see.

Human trafficking.

SIX

All sound disappeared in that moment and my vision tunneled until all I could see were those two words. *Human trafficking*. It had to be a mistake. I didn't know much about Jacquie's brother, but I had to believe there was no way he would get involved in something as heinous as that. Slowly, sound came rushing back, bringing with it a pounding headache in my temples.

"Pull up anything you can find on Jamal DeWitt." Molly recovered her senses faster than I did.

Avery's fingers hovered above the keyboard for a moment as she hesitated. She'd known Jacquie as long as I had. She, too, bore some loyalty to the woman and I doubted she wanted to be the bearer of this news. After a beat, she regained her composure and began typing away.

"There's not much here. Just says he was a person of interest and that there was an arrest a few years ago."

"What for?" I blurted.

Avery moved the cursor to a line in the electronic file, so I could see it. Only I didn't recognize the codes. I turned to Molly and offered her a questioning look. Maybe she would know what was going on.

"Looks like solicitation charges, but I don't see why they would be linked to an FBI case. That seems more tied to the local level."

"Maybe there was some sort of joint taskforce?" I suggested.

"Not a bad thought. We'll swing by Major Crimes on our way back to headquarters and see if there's anything else we can dig up," Molly replied, pulling her phone out as if to check the time. Or to see if she'd missed any calls.

"We should fill Jacquie and Duncan in on what we've found," I urged.

"We will, but there are a few other people I'd like to talk to first," she answered.

"I found the lead agent's name," Avery said,

scribbling something down on a notepad and handing it over.

"Thanks." Molly tore the page off the notepad before handing it back.

There had to be more information we could glean from the case file now that we'd brute forced our way in. "Mind if I take a look?" I gestured to the chair in which Avery sat.

"Go for it."

I settled into the chair and began skimming through the contents of the folder. I noted that the case was marked as 'Active,' even though it had events logged going back five years. How had Jamal gotten mixed up in all this? His murder wasn't the end of the story. I clicked through some of the case notes to find references to covertly recorded meetings, dates, and times. Some of the information looked vaguely familiar.

"We should get going," Molly announced. "Avery, do me a favor and send me an encrypted copy of this file. Something tells me the lead agent isn't going to be keen to share and we can't afford to lose access."

"And here I thought you were all about interdepartmental cooperation," Avery muttered before ushering me out of her chair.

I checked my own phone as we headed back through the Council Chamber room. It was closing in on noon already and I couldn't shake the sense we were running up against an invisible clock. I was halfway down the staircase to the first floor when it hit me. We'd been so focused on the vision of Jamal; we'd been completely ignoring the part of the vision that was warning us that someone else was in danger.

"Wait for me in the car. I need to do one thing," I called down to Molly before pivoting on the stairs and racing back to the tech hub.

"I need one more favor," I said, barging back into the space.

"You know, one day I'm going to decide I've had enough of being the magical world's go-to IT girl and up and leave," she noted.

"It's a quick favor, I swear," I said before launching into an explanation. "So, Neveah saw someone else in her vision last night. And I was hoping if I could show you what they look like, you could I don't know ... use your magic to run a search to tell us who she is?"

Avery spun to face me and stared with what I could only describe as amusement on her face. Her eyes brightened behind the lenses of her glasses and she even tugged her trademark headphones from around her neck.

"I've never done that before, but if you think it will help, I'll give it a try."

"Thank you. I really do owe you one," I said, relief flooding every pore in my body.

"Did you get a good look at this person?"

"Not exactly, but I think I have a work around." I extended a hand. "It will be easier if I bring you along."

She stood and accepted my hand. My magic rose off me like a perfume. Chamomile filled my nose as I tried to pull up the image of the woman in the car. I could taste something sharp on my tongue as Avery squeezed my hand. It grew stronger until my taste buds recognized it as cinnamon. For once my magic wasn't in defense mode and recognized Avery's signal boost for what it was. I exhaled and closed my eyes. The image I'd been trying to recall materialized in my head and I did my best to detach myself from it. I needed to get the best angle for Avery to use. Avery's power continued to pour into me and the car rippled. I found myself on the outside of the car, staring at the woman's face.

"Try to hold it there," Avery's voice floated to me,

as if she were miles away instead of standing beside me.

I was aware of her sketching a rough square shape around the woman's face in the windshield. When I blinked, the woman's face had vanished from the memory. In that moment, I felt Avery's hand release mine and the tiny tech space came flooding back. I steadied myself against the nearby desk and opened my eyes to find the image she'd 'snapped' from the memory somehow loaded onto her computer. I could see her running multiple facial recognition systems.

"I'll call you if something comes up," Avery answered.

"Thanks again."

My magic hung around me like a cloud as I descended the stairs to find Molly waiting out on the front steps to the building. She cast a sideways look my direction. "A minute, huh?"

"Sorry, I realized I'd forgotten to give her some information."

"What information would that be?"

"The woman who Neveah saw. I've got Avery trying to identify her. Maybe if we know who she is, we can figure out how Jamal fits into all of this."

"Good thinking."

"We have to be missing something, right? I mean Jacquie wouldn't have missed that her brother had been picked up on such serious charges, would she?"

"She did say she was focused on getting her career off the ground. And I could see why she'd want to distance herself from a relative who was making such big mistakes," Molly answered.

"So where to first? Talking to the lead agent or visiting Jacquie's old stomping grounds?"

"Better to start with the FBI," Molly replied, pressing the gas pedal to the floor.

"I know I'm still new to all of this, but is it normal to have such a heavily protected case file?"

"No, it's not. My only thought is whatever is going on, whoever is being investigated ... the bureau has someone undercover in their ranks and they're trying to compartmentalize as much as possible to protect that person's identity."

"If Jamal was picked up for solicitation it could be he tried to pick up their undercover agent," I noted. "But he was married with kids."

"He wouldn't be the first guy to stray from his marriage into the arms of someone who would accept payment for their company," Molly retorted.

I didn't disagree with her statement, but something still didn't fit with what I'd seen in Neveah's vision or the documents we'd recovered from his car. He'd clearly been gathering information for *someone*. It was looking more like he was working with the FBI after all. Had they offered him a deal to work as a confidential informant?

"I still don't understand why now, all of a sudden five years later, we're being turned on to this case," I muttered.

"I've learned not to argue with magic, much as I wish I could. If it throws something in our path, there's usually some cosmically important reason."

We made it back to downtown Boston just after noon. My stomach burbled with hunger, but I ignored the urge. We had more important things to deal with. I could eat when this case was over.

I followed Molly inside and we got off the elevator on a different floor than our usual one. She marched down the short grey corridor like she owned the place and stopped short at a nondescript doorway with a keypad.

"Uh, not to rain on this parade, but I'm pretty sure the agents in there are going to ask how we found out about their top secret human trafficking investigation and I'm pretty sure they aren't going to buy 'because of magic,'" I noted.

Molly faltered as she considered my words.

"You're not wrong." She pointed to the keypad, "And I wasn't exactly expecting this level of security."

I grinned. "Oh, that's not a problem. I could get us through no problem. But again, I have to believe they're not going to be happy to see two people who aren't supposed to be in there just pop up without having the right codes."

"Guess we need to be diplomatic," Molly muttered and pulled out her cell phone.

"What does that mean exactly?"

She smirked. "It means we need to figure out if the lead agent's even in there."

"You want me to sneak in and see who picks up your phone call."

"Use the skills you've got, right?"

I wasn't sure what she hoped to gain with this venture, but I wasn't going to argue with her. Going in solo and staying invisible was a better plan than magically appearing behind a locked door. I waited long enough to see Molly dial a number and press the phone to her ear. She held up the piece of paper from Avery, giving me the same information she had: Philomena Herrera. At least I knew what name to look for now.

I stepped up to the secured doorway and focused. I could have gone through the wall, but I had no idea what lay beyond it and no desire to get stuck. My magic fought me just a little as I reached for it.

Come on, this is your bread and butter.

I'd spent years ruled by my magic's desire to hide me away from the world. I shouldn't have to fight this hard to give it what it longed for. As I watched my extremities finally turned translucent and then vanished, an ache started at the base of my skull. Apparently J.T.'s wonder pills had a short half-life. I pushed through the discomfort and phased through the door.

Lucky for me, no one was about to leave so I didn't have to worry about accidentally passing through another person. I'd done that once before and only once. It was the weirdest fucking sensation I'd ever experienced. The interior of the office wasn't dissimilar from ours with its drab grey cubicles and offices lining the far wall. I made my way between rows of prefab desks and scanned the nameplates until I found one marked Philomena Herrera. The door sat ajar, but the lights inside were off. I was about to pass through the door when I heard the phone ring. It rang five times before stopping, likely sending the caller—hopefully Molly—to voicemail. Still, maybe this was an opportunity in disguise. I could snoop in the agent's office and see what I find.

The rest of the office space sounded empty, so I didn't bother passing through her already-open door. I allowed myself to return to corporeal form and nudged the door open. The space was sparsely decorated, with only a picture of two women standing on the steps of City Hall. Neither woman looked like the one I'd seen from Neveah's vision.

Philomena's desk drawers offered up no hints either. There was one cabinet secured with a lock and key that I could have bypassed if I was so inclined. But I didn't get the chance. Just as I'd bent to examine the drawer, feeling beneath the keyboard tray for the key, my phone vibrated in my pocket.

I glanced at the screen to see a text from Molly. Hastily pressing my finger to the screen, I opened the message to find three words: **'Get out now.'** Her message made my throat go dry and I hurried back into the open area of the office, doing my best to return Philomena's door to the same degree it had been open before I'd entered.

This time, my magic rippled around me and hid me away from the world long enough for me to run headlong at the door and pass through. I turned corporeal just in time to slam into Molly.

"What's wrong?" I demanded as she caught my arm and dragged me down the corridor away from the office.

"Jacquie just called. Neveah had another vision of the woman you saw."

"Did she get any more details about who she is or why whoever murdered Jamal is after her?"

"No. But she saw the date it is supposed to happen."

I'd never heard of a prophecy actually providing a specific date. Sure, the prophecy Ezri prevented a couple years ago had given hints about the specific conditions, but it hadn't come out and said anything like a month and day, let alone a year. I'd wondered if that was just the nature of visions and prophecies. They were meant to be purposely vague.

I found my voice again. "When?"

"August twelfth."

I stared at her. We had 48 hours to piece together why someone had wanted Jamal dead and save a stranger's life. Fan-fucking-tastic.

SEVEN

Reconvening in our office seemed the easiest solution. At the very least, it gave us privacy. I paced the length of the conference room as we waited for Jacquie and Duncan to return.

"You're sure you didn't see anything that might give us a hint about what's going on?" Molly asked for the third time since we'd returned from our trip upstairs.

"Nothing. I mean, there was a locked drawer, but I didn't have time do any extra snooping." I raked my fingers through my hair. "Are you absolutely sure we can't just, I don't know, put in a request for the records in their case? Or at least send an email saying, 'Hey, we think we have information on your case, want some help?'"

"And how exactly would we explain the way we came upon this information? I'm pretty sure a clairvoyant teenager won't fly."

I let out a groan. She wasn't wrong. But all of this intra-agency secrecy was giving me a migraine. We all wanted the same thing—to save lives. It shouldn't be this hard to accomplish that goal.

"I understand you're frustrated. Believe me, so am I," Molly noted, moving to block my path from the far wall to the whiteboard on the opposite wall.

"What about the file that Avery unlocked for us? There's got to be more in it than just an ominous reference to human trafficking."

"What unlocked file?" Jacquie's voice filtered in from just beyond the conference room door.

"Avery did her tech wizardry and was able to access the file we found. We were just about to do a deep dive," Molly answered.

"What about Jamal's phone we found in police evidence?" Duncan stepped into the room.

"She's still working on it. The thing had no power for years," I reminded him.

"It sounds like we've got a lot to fill each other in on," Jacquie said, her voice tired.

"How about I go grab us some lunch," Duncan offered.

"Why don't you go with him?" Jacquie suggested.

I was about to protest when I caught the look on her face, evoking our conversation at Notre Dame. I needed to sort this romance shit out now.

"Sure," I sighed and followed Duncan back outside.

We headed down to street level and I spotted a few food trucks setting up just outside of City Hall. I headed directly for one and got in line.

"You want to tell me why I needed an escort to pick up lunch?" Duncan stepped up beside me.

"What? You don't." I answered. "But four hands are better than two."

"I saw the look Jacquie gave you. I'm not blind, Kayla. What's going on?"

I swallowed the lump in my throat. "I'm not exactly great at relationships. I mean, my last one ended because he needed to find himself," I began. "And you're a great guy, but I don't know if I'm really ready for something serious."

"Why didn't you say something?" His voice was barely above a whisper.

"Because I also kind of suck at personal confrontation," I replied, taking a shuffling step forward.

"I think you are an amazing person, Kayla, and not just because of what you can do," he said. "If you're not ready for something serious, I understand. But you should have told me."

"Yeah, but we work together and I didn't want to screw that up. And honestly, I'm not some perfect girl. I've done things I'm not proud of."

"We all make mistakes."

"You know it's more than just mistakes," I corrected.

"Doesn't matter to me. They are part of what makes you who you are and that's the person I'm falling for. So, I wouldn't change a thing. And I can wait."

"You going to order?" a nasally male voice interrupted from inside the food truck's open window.

I cleared my throat and placed our order, stepping out of line to wait. Duncan trailed me. "I feel like I don't deserve you being so understanding," I murmured.

"I'm an easy going guy, Kayla and the best things in life are worth waiting for."

My cheeks flushed in embarrassment. I wasn't used to anyone telling me I was that important to them. I felt my magic aching to respond, to give me an out in the situation, but clamped down on it. I wasn't running away from this.

"So, uh ... did you get anything else from Troy and Neveah about when Jamal went away and where he might have gone?"

Duncan offered a smirk. "Nice way to change the subject."

"Question still stands," I replied as the vendor waved at us and gestured to our order sitting on the counter.

I snatched it up while Duncan grabbed utensils and napkins. We retreated back inside before he answered.

"They had a couple of little knick-knacks that they could clearly identify as being from these trips. One was a figurine from Rockefeller Center. There was some memorabilia from Philly too."

"Was Denise any help?"

Duncan let out a derisive snort. "She wouldn't even talk to us about it. She's trying to act like none of this is happening."

"You would think she'd want to know what happened to her husband," I muttered.

Jacquie stepped into the room, casting a disapproving look at both of us. "Denise has struggled for years with addiction and I know a lot of it stemmed from losing Jamal. I can't say I blame her for not wanting to dig up memories that might trigger her."

"But it's not fair to put all of this on her kids," I argued.

"They're stronger than a lot of adults," Jacquie answered. "But we now know where he was going and when. If Avery can unlock his phone, maybe we can figure out what he was really doing."

"I hate to have to push your sister-in-law's buttons, but knowing how he went from a solicitation charge at the state level to being swept up in a federal human trafficking case would help us figure out why this woman is being targeted," Molly noted.

"Maybe we don't need to talk to Denise," Jacquie replied. She pointed to me then to the doorway behind her. "Come on, we'll eat on the way."

I didn't argue, simply followed her down to street level. She climbed behind the wheel of her car and I dutifully slid into the passenger seat. If she wanted to fill me in on what she was thinking, she would.

"I didn't mean to imply Denise was purposely being unhelpful earlier," I said, my discomfort with the silence between us forcing me to speak.

"You had a point," Jacquie responded, merging into the light traffic passing through the center of the city at lunch time. "Maybe I'm coddling her too much, because I know what happens when she can't keep her shit together."

The way she sighed at the end and her mouth hanging open, telegraphed she wanted to say more. She stayed quiet. She expertly dipped her fork into her food carton as we stopped at red lights. I ate quickly, still trying to connect all the disparate pieces of information we'd gleaned in the last twenty-four hours.

"How is Neveah holding up after seeing a woman's potential murder?"

"Like I said, she's stronger than some adults I know. But I also know it isn't completely rolling off her. She feels such a responsibility, holding all this in her head."

"And the person she could have talked to about it is gone," I noted darkly.

"Being around other people who understand her power helps, too," Jacquie replied as she pulled into the Major Crimes precinct of the Boston Police Department—her old stomping grounds. Our destination made sense now.

"You really think they'd be willing to share more files with us?" I probed as we left the car behind.

"We're not going to be asking for files," Jacquie answered and pulled out her phone. She flicked past a few screens before she marched straight through the bullpen to the captain's office.

The woman I'd seen hand over Jamal's accident file sat behind the desk. She looked up at our unannounced entrance. "DeWitt, twice in as many days. That's got to be a record."

"Things are evolving. I need to talk to a couple of your officers," Jacquie replied.

"You know I'm always happy to help the FBI, but I'm going to need more information than that." The way her brow knit together; I could tell her words didn't actually match the sentiment.

Jacquie held up her phone and showed it to the captain. I watched the exchange. It had been a much different dynamic last night. Did Jacquie's former boss know something? Or was she just not happy about us barging into her house demanding things? I couldn't say I blamed her for the last one.

"Both of these officers are working a beat down by the Prudential Center right now," the captain replied.

Jacquie snatched the phone back before the other woman had time to take notice of the fact the electronic file she'd shown her related to Jamal. "That's all I needed. Thanks, Captain," Jacquie said.

"I really hope whatever is going on here, it works out," the captain noted.

"Me, too, ma'am," Jacquie answered.

I led the way toward the bullpen and waited until we were back to the car before speaking. "You could have gotten that information without me."

"She needed to know it wasn't just me asking this time," Jacquie said and opened the driver side door.

I shook my head, but climbed into the car and stayed silent until we found a spot near the Prudential Mall. It wasn't as bustling as I would have expected on a summer afternoon. But then again, most people's lunch hour was winding down, the call of their day jobs luring them back to the grind.

I spotted two uniformed officers standing by one of the newer entrances to the mall. I hadn't been here in forever, but thought it now led to an athletics apparel retailer. The high end kind. It explained why there might be a police presence.

"You don't really expect them to remember what happened with a guy five years ago, do you?" I whispered to Jacquie as we approached.

"We're going to find out." She passed me her phone with the case file information still open.

"Afternoon, miss," one of the officers—his nameplate read Fontana—greeted me.

I bristled at the diminutive way he addressed me, making sure I moved my badge so it was more prominently displayed on my hip. "Hoping we could speak to you and your partner," I said, using the most authoritative tone I could.

Out of the corner of my eye, I caught Jacquie hanging back. She'd found this lead, but she wanted to see how I handled interfacing with local law enforcement. Officer Fontana straightened the moment he spotted my credentials.

"Happy to help if we can, agent."

That's better.

"We were hoping you might remember this man," I said, flashing the screen so he could see Jamal's picture along with the note about the solicitation charge.

Officer Fontana squinted at the image and nudged his partner—Officer Brooks—in the chest to gain his attention. They both studied the information and slowly recognition dawned on Brooks' face.

"I can't believe I remember this guy. But it was weird. He kept insisting he wasn't soliciting. Said he was giving money to a woman who needed help getting out of a bad relationship ... he was passing it off on the street, because he didn't want the boyfriend catching wind."

"And you didn't believe him?" I noted, irritation coloring my tone.

"He was in a known area where pandering and solicitation happens," Brooks continued. "I didn't think it was going to stick."

"But remember, before we could book him, that scary FBI broad showed up," Fontana said, his cheeks flushing when he glanced my way. "Sorry, that agent."

This was getting interesting. "What agent?"

"Don't remember her name. It was something Spanish sounding," Fontana rambled.

"Herrera?" I supplied hopefully.

"Might be. She insisted that we should bury the case, that she'd take over."

It certainly fit with our working theory that Jamal had somehow ended up as an informant with the FBI. "You work that area where you arrested him a lot?"

"Used to. It's cleaned up in the last few years."

"Did you ever suspect anything more nefarious was happening? Girls and women being forced into soliciting?" I pressed.

Both men shook their heads at my question, their eyes going wide at the suggestion that they'd missed something big going on right under their noses. I wasn't going to get anything more from either of them.

"Thank you gentlemen," I said and pivoted on my heel.

"Something happen to this guy or something?" Fontana called after me.

"Sorry, can't discuss an ongoing investigation," I called over my shoulder and retreated to the car.

I contained myself until Jacquie closed the driver side door. "Okay, that felt kind of amazing."

"Having been on the receiving end of that power play, it isn't fun. But you nailed it," Jacquie praised with a small half-smile. I'd take it.

"Does Jamal helping a friend get out of a bad situation sound like it fits?"

"More so than him stepping out on Denise. Even when she was hitting rock bottom, he was always there for her."

"And this is another connection to Agent Herrera. She wasn't there when I slipped into her office."

I spotted Jacquie's arched brow in the rearview mirror before she turned her attention on pulling into the flow of traffic again. "Do I want to know how you got in?"

I grinned. "Did you forget I can walk through walls?"

"Find anything interesting?"

Before I could respond, Jacquie's phone rang with an incoming call from Molly. She tapped the screen.

"On our way back now. What's wrong?"

"Oh, you know, just getting angry visits from other members of the Bureau," Molly answered.

Jacquie flipped on the siren and pressed her foot to the gas pedal. We reached FBI headquarters in five minutes flat. If I hadn't known she didn't have a drop of magic in her body, I'd have assumed she bent the laws of physics to make the trip faster. We made it into the conference room just in time to see a slender woman with slicked back dark brown hair storm in behind us. She towered over Molly and I, but matched Jacquie in height. Even still, I could see the unease in Jacquie's demeanor.

"Who is in charge?" the newcomer demanded. None of us needed to ask who she was.

"That would be me," Molly replied sounding far more confident than I would have.

"You want to tell me why the hell you've been sniffing around my investigation?"

The tension in the room thickened the longer Molly didn't answer. We couldn't just tell her we'd found years old evidence on the say-so of a clairvoyant teenager. Sure, we knew about magic, but there was absolutely nothing to suggest Agent Herrera was aware of its existence.

"That case file is heavily encrypted for a reason," Agent Herrera continued, apparently unmoved by the fact she hadn't gotten an answer to her question.

"You act like you're the only one in this agency with sensitive case information," Molly finally answered.

"Tell me why you're looking into this," Herrera repeated.

"It's complicated," I blurted.

All eyes fell on me and I regretted opening my mouth. I had no idea what I was going to say to make this woman back down or how I was going to keep magic a secret from her. But there was no going back now.

"Un-complicate it," Herrera said coolly.

Casting my co-workers, a plaintive look, I sucked in a breath. "We weren't looking into your case. Not initially. See, we got some information about a death that occurred a few years ago. It had been ruled an accident, but we have reason to believe it occurred under suspicious circumstances."

"Sounds like a local jurisdiction issue," Herrera noted dismissively.

"Your local jurisdiction issue was my brother," Jacquie interjected, drawing the other woman's attention. "Jamal DeWitt."

Herrera's complexion paled at the mention of his name. "What makes you think his death wasn't accident?"

Jacquie shook her head, arms crossed over her chest in a defiant stance. "No. You don't walk into our office demanding answers. I want to know why you scooped him up on a bogus solicitation charge.

What does my brother have to do with human trafficking?"

The bravado melted out of Agent Herrera's posture. "I really am not at liberty to discuss the details of my investigation."

"Maybe we could help you?" I offered in a soft tone. "Please, tell us what he was involved in. It might help us solve our case."

"Jamal's been dead for five years," Herrera noted.

"Like she said, we have reason to believe it occurred under suspicious circumstances. And I'm guessing if he was wrapped up with some hush-hush FBI investigation, that might have been a motive," Jacquie replied.

"No one knew he was working with us. We were careful about that," Herrera insisted.

"Someone knew," I countered. "And they forced him off the road."

"If I told you the nature of our investigation, you would think I'm insane," the other agent whispered.

I was about to tell her we'd seen some seriously fucked up stuff, but realized that wasn't the right way to approach the situation or to speak to a superior. "We've seen more than you might think," I finally noted.

"We've been trying to trace the head of a nation-wide ring. They take mostly young women and girls in major metropolitan areas. But as far as we can tell, the girls they're recruiting go willingly."

"Are they kids off the street? People who might be more willing to go with the promise of a warm meal and a bed?" I pressed.

"Of those we've been able to identify, which isn't as many as we'd like, most came from decent homes."

"So not your typical mark for this sort of thing," I murmured. "But what's so crazy about that?"

"Because we think they're using ... magic."

The four of us all stared at Agent Herrera in stunned silence. I knew what I'd heard the woman say. I caught Molly and then Duncan's gazes. They nodded, as if to say 'yeah, I heard it, too.'

"That is not where I thought this was going," I sighed. "But it makes a lot more sense when you factor in what we know."

"You actually believe me?" Herrera's brows inched up toward her hairline.

Jacquie moved before anyone could speak, shutting the door to the conference room and pulling the blinds even though we were the only ones in the office.

"What are you doing?" Herrera demanded.

"Making a point," Jacquie quipped and pointed to me.

I was starting to feel a bit like a one-trick pony, dragged out to impress the tourists. But I didn't argue. Instead, I closed my eyes, letting my magic wash over me. By Herrera's sharp intake of breath, I knew my magic had responded as intended. I'd vanished.

"So, how about we stop waving our dicks around and figure out how we can help each other," I said, rematerializing. I caught Molly's disapproving look, but shrugged.

Agent Herrera turned to look at Jacquie first. "I can't just read you in. There's been so much work put into this and our network of agents is small for a reason." She started to pace around the perimeter of the rectangular table taking up the main space of the room. "If I'm being honest, I thought Jamal's death seemed off. But the medical examiner had ruled it an accident due to a seizure and who was I to argue."

"We located his car. He had documents he was trying to bring to you," Molly said calmly.

"And how do you know he was planning to bring them here?"

"Because we saw his GPS," Duncan continued.

"How?"

"Magic," I replied bluntly. "Like I said, we got information that led us to reexamine his death and we learned that something magical was responsible for running him off the road."

"I understand if you can't fully read us in, but please, tell me how my brother fit into all of this. We spoke with the arresting officers on the soliciting charge. They said you just swooped in and told them to bury the charges."

"We had a few locations under surveillance as possible hunting grounds. He got too close and we needed to know what he'd seen. Once we explained what was going on, he offered to help."

"By going to nearby cities and scoping them out," I extrapolated.

"Yes. But how could you know that?"

"He brought souvenirs home to his children," Jacquie replied.

"He shouldn't have done that," Herrera sighed.

"Did his trips turn up anything actionable?" I pressed.

"Until you get cleared, I can't tell you that." She rubbed at her temples. "I need to know why all of a sudden you're looking into Jamal's death."

"It's not just him," Molly offered. "We have

reason to believe that someone else may be in danger. A woman. We don't know her identity yet, but we do know we've only got a few days to stop whoever is behind this ring from killing her, too."

"How much time?" Herrera stopped her pacing, hands fidgeting on the back of the nearest chair.

"Two days," I answered.

Even more color drained from the agent's face as she squeezed the back of the chair tight. I tried to fit the pieces together. There was the potential that people with magic were luring suburban girls and women into sexual servitude. But how were they doing it?

"Can I ask you one thing?" I stepped up beside the woman. "Does the name Order of Samael ring any bells?"

Agent Herrera shook her head. "Doesn't sound familiar. Why?"

"Just covering all of our bases."

"I will see what I can do about getting you clearance to be read into the investigation. And then I'm going to need to know exactly what you found." Herrera released her grip on the chair in front of her and pivoted toward the still-closed door.

"Agent Herrera, out of curiosity, how did you

know we were looking into your case?" I moved to block her exit.

"It wasn't a coincidence the same agent who tried to access the case file, then called me," she replied. Her lips quirked into the ghost of a smirk. "And last I checked, office doors don't have a habit of opening and closing on their own in a locked environment.

"You knew about my magic," I said, my voice deflated.

"Not you specifically. But given what we suspect about the ring we're chasing; it isn't out of the realm of possibility."

"Guess being able to turn invisible isn't completely fool-proof," I sighed.

Herrera gestured to the door behind me. "As you noted, we have a deadline we're running up against. The sooner I can get you clearance, the sooner we can both get what we want."

I stepped out of her way and took a steadying breath. It made sense there were other agents in the bureau who knew about magic, but somehow I hadn't anticipated working with them. As Agent Herrera left the conference room behind, a new thought popped into my head.

"We should check with Authority records. They

might know if anyone has gone missing. I mean they knew about when Neveah and the other girls disappeared," I said, eyeing Jacquie.

"It's worth a shot, but do you have any way to get in touch with or sway the Council?" Duncan interjected. When I arched a brow at him in surprise, he shrugged. "I pick up on things."

"The Council isn't some unapproachable, faceless entity. I know someone who might be able to help."

I hated having to ask J.T. for help again so soon. Despite that I hoped the potential crisis would be enough to secure his assistance and his innate nature to help those around him. Besides, it gave me a reason to check in with Avery to see if she'd found anything on our mystery woman or anything else that might help lead to unraveling a magical human trafficking ring on Jamal's phone.

"Why don't I join you?" Molly said.

"I think I can handle an Authority visit on my own," I protested.

"We're going to need all eyes on this." She turned to look at Jacquie. "We aren't going to wait for Agent Herrera to give us her blessing. Start digging into their files. The sooner we figure out who the players are, the sooner we can get some damn justice for Jamal."

I let her take the lead down to the car and slid into the passenger seat. She'd been to Authority Headquarters enough over the last few years to be behind the wheel.

"You're checking up on me," I said as she pulled into mid-afternoon city traffic.

"Wouldn't be doing my job otherwise," she said. "I'm your superior. If I'm not making sure my people are okay, mentally and physically, then I'm putting everyone on this team at risk."

"I pushed myself a little, but I'll be fine. It's nothing I can't handle," I answered just as a twinge started over the bridge of my nose.

"No one expects you to be Ezri," she said bluntly, catching me off guard.

"I don't think I need to be her," I said defensively.

"Could have fooled me. Those spells you did yesterday were things she would have tried. And no offense, but she was a lot more powerful than you. And it would have worn her out, too."

"I went into this line of work, because she inspired me to make amends for my past mistakes.

But what good am I if I can't even use my magic to help fix things for other people."

"I hate to tell you this, but most of the world gets along just fine without magic. We rely on each other to help us break through the tough times."

"I just feel like if I can't even manage to tough out a few headaches, I'm not doing her legacy justice."

"She might not have told you that you're being too hard on yourself, but Desmond absolutely would."

I couldn't help but laugh at that. She was right. He'd admonish me on the spot for not taking care of myself and pushing myself past my limits. "It still hits me sometimes, how hard it is to do all of this without them both."

"Just because they aren't here doesn't mean they aren't still with us," Molly said.

"That's not how magic works," I corrected. In fact, I'd learned from Ezri and Desmond that magic gets reabsorbed by the world when a bloodline dies and is reborn into a new one. But the magic isn't the same and it's never quite as strong. Ezri and Des were the exceptions.

"You know, you weren't wrong to wonder if the Order was involved," Molly continued.

"It just doesn't seem like their M.O. Sure they kidnapped a few kids, but that wasn't anything sexual."

"They don't have a monopoly on being evil assholes."

In some small way it had almost been comforting to think the Order were the only magical bad guys roaming the streets of Boston. They were a familiar enemy and one that had been sufficiently defanged in recent months. To know there were people out there using their abilities to subvert innocent people's wills sent chills down my spine.

"I hate feeling like we're so many steps behind," I groaned as the circular drive and the austere exterior of Authority Headquarters came into view.

"Something tells me they didn't count on a teenager having a vision that would point us squarely in their direction. They might know about Herrera and her investigation, but they don't know about us."

We're the wild card.

We pulled into the driveway just as the front doors opened and J.T. appeared on the front steps. The worry lines etched on his face were visible even from this distance. He was either still concerned about Neveah or he knew something we didn't. Neither option thrilled me.

I was out of the car before Molly could put it in park and cut the engine. J.T. met me halfway down the front steps.

"I thought you might be coming," he said.

"Did Neveah see something else?"

"No. But Avery let something slip about some top-secret human trafficking case. I've always been better at healing physical ailments, but I'll do what I can for the mental trauma."

"I'll keep that in mind. But right now, we need your pull on the Council," I answered.

"The Council? Why?"

"Because we need to know if any of the trafficking victims had magic and you're the only person we trust enough to make our case. We hoped you'd be able to help us sift through any missing person reports folks might have filed."

"I don't hold as much sway as you think, but anything I can do to help." I could see the sadness in his expression. There was more he wanted to say about why he lacked pull, but he kept it to himself. My brain unhelpfully tried to fill in the blank with the fact he'd been married to the Savior for only a day.

"That's all we ask," Molly interjected.

We turned to head inside when the echo of

hurried footfalls on the stairs inside stopped us short. Avery appeared looking frantic. She had her phone half raised to her ear. I felt my phone buzz once in my pocket before she lowered it, ending the call she didn't need to make.

"I just got an ID on your mystery woman."

NINE

J.T., Molly, and I followed Avery inside. Our footsteps thudded on the carpeted staircase up to the top level. I caught a glimpse of J.T. out of the corner of my eye as he cast a look at the Council Chamber before we passed through into the tech hub. Thoughts about how he was going to convince the rest of the Council to help us no doubt weighed on him. The screens on the desk were a jumble of information. I could see that by some miracle—and probably a little magic—she'd revived the battery on Jamal's phone, too. Avery flitted from the keyboard to the phone, to another machine, and back again without speaking.

"I appreciate the urgency with letting us know you cracked the identity of our mystery woman, but why are you so freaked out?" I said, trying to pull her focus back to the reason she'd come to find us.

"Sorry, just one second," she mumbled, fingers flying over the keys.

"Is she okay?" Molly stage whispered.

"No idea," I answered.

"Hey, Avery, what's going on?" J.T.'s voice was soft, soothing almost.

The tension in Avery's shoulders relaxed and I could sense what almost felt like a guided air current pass by me and hit her directly. I closed my eyes, inhaled, and reached inward for just a sliver of power. Just enough to open my eyes to the magic around us and see what might be hiding. Sure enough, there was an invisible current pulsing from J.T.'s hand, flowing straight to Avery. He was using his healing gifts to help her calm down and focus.

"We had a breach," she said, her voice slow.

"I think that might have been our fault," Molly said, stepping up to place a hand on Avery's shoulder. "I didn't realize that the agents we were dealing with knew about magic and might think to look for any sort of intrusion that way."

Avery sunk into her seat. "I thought I'd gotten sloppy or distracted."

"You haven't been taking much time off have you?" There was no judgment in J.T.'s question.

"This is what I'm good at. This is what I can do to help people. This is what ..." she trailed off.

"What you think Desmond would want you to do," I finished for her and she nodded.

"I know we didn't know him in the same way, but I know for sure he wouldn't want you pushing yourself to the point of exhaustion. You don't owe anyone any of this." I waved a hand at the space around us.

"It's going to sound stupid, but I never felt really seen here ... until Ezri walked through that door with that magically corrupted video footage."

"Come on, everyone knew you were the best tech whiz here," J.T. said with a smile.

"I felt useful when it actually helped catch the bad guy, but I'd be lying if I didn't admit seeing all the dark shit you guys deal with doesn't mess me up."

I wanted to tell her she didn't have to feel obligated to help us, but if I was being honest, I wouldn't know where else to turn. She was just that good and reliable, and we could trust her.

"It screws me up, too," I said instead. "And I'm not that great at dealing with it either."

"Thanks," she said softly and adjusted her glasses.

"Promise me you're going to start taking time for yourself," J.T. said, his tone taking on a stern quality.

"I promise," she said, miming crossing her heart.

"Now, what did you find on our mystery woman?" Molly said, nudging her back on task.

Avery hastily exited out of various program windows before pulling up an image that I thought looked like the woman I'd seen in Neveah's vision. Even though I hadn't gotten that good of a look at her. There was something in the facial structure and eyes that looked familiar that I couldn't place.

"Meet Constanza Valez," Avery said. "She's from just outside of D.C. originally. Looks like she moved to Quincy about six months ago. Works as a beautician at a salon here in the city."

"Any criminal history?" I asked.

"Not unless you count a couple parking tickets and one jaywalking citation."

"Not someone who screams easy pickings for a trafficking operation," Molly murmured.

"But she seems to fit the profile of what Agent Herrera said these assholes were targeting. Suburban middle class women and girls."

"That still doesn't explain why, if we're right and

the same person or entity that forced Jamal off the road, is targeting her."

"Maybe she got scooped up by Herrera?" I suggested.

"It's possible. Or maybe their abduction goes wrong and she's collateral damage?"

There was every possibility she was their next target. We needed to start digging into whether any of the other known victims were practitioners or not. "Does the Authority have electronic records of everyone under their purview?"

"Uh, it's nothing official and I'm pretty sure it's out of date by a few decades, but we do have some records. Why?"

"Because they're trying to figure out if any of the people who've been trafficked had magic," J.T. filled in.

"I'll see what I can find. I don't think Constanza is in the records, even if she's got magic. I mean, unless she had brushes with the Authority for some reason. It's not like they can just track people who show up in the city. I know magic can do almost anything, but I have seen no evidence that they've used their powers that way."

I hadn't seen anything like that either. For one thing, it would make existing as a Whisperer a lot harder if there were people in power who could track us simply because we had magic. Just then, Molly's phone rang with an incoming call. She stepped into the space between the meeting room and the tech hub to answer. She returned a moment later with a relieved look on her face.

"That was Agent Herrera. She came through and has given us full access to their files."

"We should run this information about Constanza by her, see if she's come up in any of their dealings. My gut tells me she's kept some things out of the file," I replied.

"The phone should be working now, too. I didn't get a chance to look through it, but the battery did charge," Avery offered, tugging the device off the charging cable.

I pocketed the phone, not sure that I wanted to be the one going through Jamal's texts and messages. It felt private, like something Jacquie ought to do on her own.

"Thank you again for the help," I told Avery before turning to face J.T. "As soon as we have more information on these missing women, I'll let you know. Maybe if we just float some names by the Council first that might make it easier."

J.T. nodded. "In the interim, I'll let them know what's going on."

I patted his arm as a thank you and followed Molly back into the Council Chamber room, then down the stairs to the front of the building. Silence descended on us as we made the trek back to FBI headquarters. I closed my eyes and tried to picture Constanza from the snippet in Neveah's vision. There had to be something else we were missing, as to why these traffickers would target her.

"You holding up?" Molly's voice pierced my focus.

"Yeah, just trying to go through what I can remember from Neveah's vision." It was frustrating how quickly the details faded and I wasn't going to make a kid relive such a traumatic accident, even if that's how her magic manifested. "And I still can't believe Jamal was working undercover with Herrera."

"It makes a lot more sense than him being involved in actual trafficking. I can't honestly believe anyone with a daughter would walk into that willingly."

"I don't mean to sound indelicate, but he's been dead for five years and their investigation is still ongoing. Either he was a terrible asset or he was the linchpin and whoever is running this crew knew it and that's why they took him out."

"We'll find out soon enough," Molly replied as we reached FBI headquarters.

Time to unravel this damn mystery before time runs out.

TEN

By the time afternoon faded into evening, images of missing women swam in my head. I felt like we were no closer to understanding what we faced than when we started. To add to my frustration, despite reading us in, Agent Herrera had not rematerialized to share information about her investigation. Jamal's cell phone sat on the table beside me. Jacquie hadn't seemed interested in sifting through its data and none of the rest of us had wanted to take the first step. But we were running out of time. We only had two days to figure out how to find and save Constanza from a currently nameless and faceless foe.

Behind me, I heard Duncan adding images and printouts to the whiteboard. I pivoted to see what he'd constructed. We'd managed to determine that there was a cyclical pattern in the rash of abductions that shifted from Boston and New York down past New Jersey and Pennsylvania. There also appeared to be dead periods in the winter months.

"What, is our mastermind a snowbird and they retire to Florida for the winter?" I grumbled in irritation.

"Not a bad thought," Duncan said, fixing me with a hopeful smile.

It did nothing to assuage my annoyance. He'd jotted down every defining characteristic of the missing women—nearly three hundred in the last five years alone—but it was too varied to even nail down a partial profile. They came from different locations, were of different ethnic backgrounds, and ranged from age sixteen all the way to twenty-five. I tried to recall the names of the some of the victims from our area, but none of them sounded familiar.

On a whim, I turned back to the conference table and scooped up Jamal's phone. I hit the home button and the screen came to life displaying a photo of Neveah and Troy. They had mugged for the camera and hot tears pricked the back of my eyes at what they'd lost, all because their father was trying to do the right thing.

I tapped the home button again, but the screen prompted me for a pass code. "Jacquie, any idea what Jamal's pin might have been?"

She passed me a sheet of paper where she'd scribbled a bunch of four digit numbers. I said a silent prayer that the system didn't lock me out after too many failed attempts and went with the first set of numbers. The phone gave a little shake to tell me I'd chosen incorrectly. I jotted down a little 'x' next to the first number.

"Jacquie, what was Jamal's birthday again?" I prompted.

"August tenth," Jacquie answered without looking up from her own file.

I checked and found the sequence of 0810 as one of the last options on the list. I entered it and the device rewarded me with the home screen full of a bunch of apps that hadn't been used or updated in years. Before I had time to start checking out his emails, texts, or notes apps, Jacquie stood, file still in hand.

"Okay, I think we've finally gotten some information we can use," she declared.

She spun on her heel and slammed a dark image in the center of Duncan's work. It was clearly a surveillance photo taken at night from a distance.

The man pictured in it was blading and sported a beard. Duncan stepped back from the board and we turned our collective attention to Jacquie.

"Nathaniel Dermott is the suspected head of this ring. He's got deep pockets with real estate holdings in several cities," Jacquie explained.

The name tickled something in the back of my mind, but I couldn't quite put my finger on what. I waited for Jacquie to continue her explanation.

"This guy is good at hiding money trails and there's been no clear connection between him and any of the missing women. He doesn't do the recruiting himself."

"That makes sense. He's like a broker," Molly noted from across the conference table. "So, we see if Jamal had any dealings with Dermott. Maybe he got too close and they figured out what he was doing and that's why they killed him."

"There's something about this guy. I can't quite explain it, but something feels familiar," I said, squinting at the image.

"Well, he's never actually been arrested, so there's nothing in either our or local law enforcement's database regarding distinguishing marks," Jacquie noted.

She really meant there was no evidence linking

him to the Order. They branded their members and that wasn't something you could easily get rid of. But for all of their chaos and sowing discord, the Order had never felt like they would subjugate people.

"He's got an office downtown in the financial district. We could pay him a visit." The look in Jacquie's eyes warned she was edging towards recklessness.

"If Herrera and her team haven't found anything to bring him in on, we can't just barge in there," Molly reminded her. "I know you want answers for Jamal, but we need to be smart about this."

"Guys," Duncan interjected. "I think I found something, too."

I turned to find him holding up a missing person's report. At first, I didn't see anything of note about it. Duncan gave an audible huff of annoyance that we weren't seeing what he had. Not until he read out the address, the latest victim had last been seen on Commonwealth Avenue near Boston University.

"Wait a minute," Molly said, the wheels turning in her head.

My mind whirred too, picturing the address in my head. "She was at Notre Dame."

Duncan jabbed his finger at the paper with a big

grin. "According to the report, she was out with some friends. They reported her missing when they went to leave and couldn't find her. One of the witnesses said they thought they saw her heading off with someone, but couldn't give a description."

"When was this?" I made a grabbing motion for the paper and he passed it over. The report said the victim, Amelia Vicenti, had last been seen a week ago.

"This is more than we had before. Good work," I told Duncan, reaching for my keys.

"Where are you off to?" Jacquie moved to bar my way.

"The last place this woman was seen is a known magical hotspot. I'm going to see what they might have missed," I answered.

"Not alone," Agent Herrera's voice said from the doorway.

I cast Molly a glance, as if to ask permission, but she nodded in silence. I let the more experienced agent lead the way down to the parking lot.

"We didn't have much luck with the owner," Herrera offered once we were on the road.

A snort slipped out before I could think better of it. "Yeah, Jonathan is not a fan of people with badges."

"Sounds like you know him."

"We have history. But I'll get him to talk to us."

BY OUTSIDE APPEARANCES, you'd never know something had happened at Notre Dame. It was just as busy as usual, with college kids lined up around the block hoping to get in.

"Explain the appeal to me," Herrera said as we approached the front door.

I stopped a good six feet from the bar and caught her arm to stop her. "Magic being real is a usually well-guarded secret, but sometimes people talk when they shouldn't. This place has a reputation for being the real deal. So, kids get curious."

"Do you think the owner had anything to do with this?"

"No. he's an asshole, sure. But he would never endanger people's lives, especially innocent people," I answered and marched up to the bouncer.

"Aren't you a bit old for a place like this?" the bouncer scoffed, eyeing Herrera.

"Let's not make assumptions," she countered. "We need to speak with the owner."

"And why would he want to speak to you?"

"Because Molly sent us and it would really help us out," I interrupted.

The bouncer rolled his eyes, but hiked his thumb toward the open door. Herrera grabbed my elbow and mouthed 'Molly?'.

"They're sort of a thing."

She didn't have time to question me further before the heavy thud of the bass overtook us. I honestly didn't know how Jonathan and his patrons didn't go deaf from the constant vibrations. I scanned the space behind the bar, finally catching the man of the hour at the far end.

"Let me take the lead on this," I said, stepping up to a free spot a few seats down from where Jonathan stood.

"Drinking alone?" he snickered before Herrera stepped up behind me. "Experimenting?"

"Don't be a dick," I quipped. "We're working. And you have information we need."

"About what?"

"A young woman went missing from here a week ago," Herrera said, stepping up beside me at the bar. "My agents report you were not interested in speaking with them at the time."

I leaned across the bar and stage whispered, "You ought to talk to her now. I'm pretty sure she can do more than just shut you down for being uncooperative."

The look on his face shifted just a little and with the way his hands stretched out across the length of the bar, I could feel him losing the slightest grip on the magic he used on a near-constant basis. I'd never gotten the courage to ask him how he managed to sustain his illusion so flawlessly. No, it wasn't courage, it was self-preservation. His condition lent him extra physical strength that no one wanted to be on the receiving end of when he lost his temper. Asking him about his magic would most likely result in some physical pain.

"Come with me," he grunted.

I slid off the bar stool and wound my way past the patrons on the dance floor. I glanced back to ensure Agent Herrera was still with us and noticed someone had already claimed our spot at the bar. Jonathan lifted up the panel separating the club from the back of the bar. He beckoned us into an office, a place I had never stepped foot in before tonight. It was sparse, with a computer sitting on a desk. A single metal file cabinet took up the space between the end of the desk and the far wall.

He caught me staring and offered up a smirk. "Expecting chaos?"

"Or something," I muttered.

"Shut the door."

Herrera eased the door closed and Jonathan turned toward the computer sitting dormant on the desk. I found myself watching the way his shoulder muscles moved, shifting beneath the magic that presented him as a hulking man with the face of a model.

"So, Mr. ..." Herrera began before trialing off when Jonathan didn't answer.

"You really think someone went missing from my bar?" he still wouldn't face us.

"We know they did. We have the report her friends filed. And it fits with a case we're working," I explained.

"Shit," he swore.

"What aren't you telling us?" I stepped around him so he had no choice but to look at me. "Come on, Jonathan. We've had our issues, but I know you wouldn't want people to get hurt on your watch. Your no magic rule stands for a reason, right?"

His jaw tensed at the mention of 'magic.' I shrugged. "We aren't the only ones in the know."

"Just what I need, more cops nosing around," he grumbled.

"Last Sunday, what can you tell us?" Herrera's tone was soft, but prodding.

"I had a feeling something was off. I may not like magic being flung around in my bar, but that doesn't mean I don't have my own defenses set up. Anyway, I got a weird feeling, but things were so busy that night, I didn't have time to check. Then cops showed up the next morning."

"You have cameras, don't you?" I noted.

"Your tech friend going to work her magic on them?" he snickered.

"I'll have you know that tech friend has helped solve more cases than you ever will," I snapped.

"You can have whatever you want."

"We think whoever took this young woman lured her by magic," Herrera continued.

"No matter how busy it was, if magic was going on in my bar, I'd have known and I'm telling you nothing like that happened."

I gestured toward the computer and mimed typing to signal he should get to sending us the footage he had for Avery to comb through. He nudged me out of the way and sat down in front of the keyboard, his fingers tapping away at a speed I'd never expect from him. He jammed a USB flash drive into the machine, dragging files onto it.

"One more question, since we're here," I noted while the files copied. "Does the name Nathaniel Dermott ring any bells?"

"She'd do this, too, you know," he muttered, the irritation clear in his tone.

"Who?" Confusion colored Herrera's tone.

"She was just doing her job," I reminded him. "And so are we. So, does the name ring any bells?"

"No. But I'm guessing if it comes up I should let you know?"

"Your government would be very grateful if you did," I answered and caught the flash drive he flung in my direction.

"Thank you for your cooperation," Herrera said and opened the office door.

"It's never easy doing the right thing," I whispered toward the man still seated at the computer. "But she'd be proud of you for doing it."

I was back in the thrum of the bass and the crowd before he could respond. I found Herrera waiting outside the bar. The line to get in had thinned as the clock ticked closer to midnight.

"Want to fill me in on whatever that was in there?"

"It's nothing," I said, pocketing the drive and heading for the car.

"I'll be frank Agent Rogers, I don't know you very well. And that makes you a liability in my book. So, you're going to tell me what that was about."

"A couple years ago, I helped out this cop ... Ezri, Jacquie's former partner actually. She was kind of a big deal in the magical world. Let's just say more than one of the cases she worked brought her to Jonathan's door step."

"That's a lot of past tense."

"She died saving the world. And we're all still trying to adjust to the world without her in it."

"Did you believe him when he said that no magic happened in there without him knowing it?"

"I do. Which means either our abductor is a hell of a lot cleverer than Jonathan or they lured our victim outside where they knew they could get her under their power."

Both options were terrifying. But there was little we could do until we saw the video footage for ourselves. And it looked like Agent Herrera would be with us for the duration. She might not trust me yet, but that went both ways. I'd answered her questions, now it was time for her to answer some of mine.

AUGUST 11, 2019

ELEVEN

We were halfway back to FBI headquarters when my phone buzzed with an incoming text from Molly with a directive to go home and get a few hours' sleep. I expected Herrera to blow off the suggestion. This was her case after all and she'd been chasing Dermott for years. But she just nodded when I read the text aloud and dropped me off at my apartment.

"How come you haven't gotten enough to nail this prick yet?" I couldn't keep the question inside any longer.

"When we lost Jamal, I honestly thought the case had died, too. But in my heart I knew this man was still hurting women and girls. So, I kept pushing and digging. Even when the brass told me in no uncertain terms to drop it."

"I can understand that." I sat with my hand on the door handle, not ready to leave.

"I know you have more questions. I don't blame you, but your supervising agent gave you an order and I'm not about to get into a pissing contest. So, go get some sleep and you have my word I will answer your questions in a few hours."

"I'm going to hold you to that," I noted before getting out of the car and making the trek up to my apartment.

I paused outside the bathroom, the pills J.T. had given me calling my name. I didn't have time to rest. We had less than two days to figure out an angle to Constanza and unearth solid proof linking Nathaniel to the trafficking ring. I could sleep when I was dead.

I settled at the table in my kitchen and pulled out my laptop. Logging into the FBI secure network, I pulled up the information on our latest victim, so I had a good reference image to work from. Pulling the flash drive from my pocket, I plugged it in and opened the footage from Jonathan. There were more cameras than I'd expected—six in total—and wasn't sure which to look at first. Finally, I spotted a young woman by the bar who matched the victim's description.

"Could you make this any more difficult?" I grumbled to myself before finding a way to show just the camera angle I needed.

I watched as she sat there at the bar. A younger guy with dark hair and a scruffy beard approached her. The friends who'd reported her missing were nowhere to be seen. Maybe she'd been the one to get their drinks and she was just waiting for the order. The newcomer sat down on the stool beside Amelia and despite not having audio, I could still see their lips move as they talked. A chill ran down my spine and settled uncomfortably in my stomach as I waited for the inevitable.

He slid something across the bar to her that looked like a business card. What was this guy playing at? Trying to zoom in on the footage only turned it grainy and unusable. I hated having to dump this on Avery's lap after everything she'd already done for us.

"It can't be that hard," I told myself. After all, it wasn't like the footage was magically corrupted or going to try and strangle me.

Probably.

I rewound the footage a few frames and paused it where the card was as visible as it could be on the surface of the bar. I swallowed my nerves and focused. My magic snapped to attention the moment I reached for it. But I was going to ask it to do something it had never done before and I wasn't entirely sure it would work.

"Okay, just imagine I'm there. I just need to see what's on that card. In and out," I said, trying to give myself a pep talk and work out my plan of attack simultaneously.

Chamomile tickled my nose as I reached out my hand to the computer screen. A spark jumped from the computer to my finger and zapped me. I let out a hiss of discomfort as the world around me disappeared. For a long moment I occupied a black void and panic tightened my chest, making it difficult to catch my breath.

Then the bar slowly materialized around me. I could see Amelia sitting at the bar in front of me and her abductor sat there looking intensely in her direction. I knew I had to get closer to find the information I needed, but my feet were glued in place.

"People are counting on you. Just pick up your feet and move," I chided.

Pushing through my nerves, I forced my feet to move, to close the brief distance between where I stood and the bar. The lighting above the bar was dim, but it was still strong enough to read by and I could make out some sort of Celtic knot looking logo on the card along with a name: Fletcher Talent Management.

The scent and feel of my magic slipped away from me as my head began to swim. It throbbed as if in time to one of the songs that always seemed to be playing at the bar and I staggered backward.

That dark void enveloped me again, but this time I was so focused on ensuring my head didn't crack open like a coconut I didn't notice the lack of oxygen sensation. Before I knew it, I was in my apartment again, sprawled laying on my back on the floor.

"Fuck," I groaned, trying to sit up.

The room around me tilted to one side and I sunk back onto the carpet, spreading my fingers out to make as much contact as possible until the dizziness passed. Apparently my magic didn't like being forced to do something aside from conceal me.

"Stupid magic."

My temples throbbed in response and I bit back another groan. Taking steady breaths, I tried sitting up again and this time the world didn't spin off its axis. Dragging myself to the chair I'd fallen from, I found the video still paused on my laptop. I hit play, massaging the space between my eyebrows as I watched Amelia study the card on the bar, glance over her shoulder, and then follow the man out of frame. I backed out of the single view and tried to track them on any of the other cameras, but they were gone. It was as if they'd just vanished into thin air.

It wasn't out of the realm of possibility, especially given the things I'd seen and experienced since my magic had turned on me. But my gut told me our guy was just good at avoiding cameras. I rewound the footage from the spot at the bar and turned my attention to our mystery man. The way he touched his ear was easy to miss the first time around. But it definitely looked like he was concealing some sort of earpiece.

This was more than we had even just a few hours ago. It was a small victory. I reached for my phone to call Molly or Jacquie and share what I'd found, but stopped short. Calling either of them at this hour, especially when Molly had decreed a few hours' rest was only going to anger them. And while the world might have stopped spinning, my head still felt like I had the world's worst hangover.

I dragged myself back to the bathroom for a half-dose of J.T.'s pills and crawled into bed.

MAYBE IT WAS the fact I only took a half-dose or maybe the ticking clock of the case was getting to me, but I tossed and turned until my alarm blared in my ear at five o'clock. The few snatches of sleep I'd managed repeated Amelia's abduction on a loop. And for some reason, Constanza had made an appearance a time or two. There had to be a connection we weren't seeing yet.

Agent Herrera had promised answers and I intended to get them. The roads were empty as I made the trip into FBI headquarters. I spotted Jacquie's car in the lot. I stepped into the conference room to find her surrounded by print outs of what appeared to be text messages and emails.

"Please tell me you haven't been here all morning," I said, easing the door shut behind me.

"Don't tell Molly," she said, reaching for a to-go cup of coffee. The way she grimaced after tasting it hinted at just how long it had been sitting there untouched.

"What is all this?"

"Everything I could pull off Jamal's phone. It took me a few hours, but I figured out the notes you found in his car. They corresponded to dates of emails and texts."

"Anything linking it specifically to Dermott?"

"Not yet." She tossed the cup in the trash and sank back in her chair. "From what I can tell, he was getting closer, though. They had him scouting out events of some sort and reporting back on potential talent."

Talent.

I picked up one of the emails sitting on the table and saw an email address ending with ftm.com. "Was it for Fletcher Talent Management?"

"Uh, maybe." She scanned a few other pages littering the table. "Yes. How did you know that?"

"You weren't the only one doing a little after hours investigating." My temples twinged as a reminder. "We convinced Jonathan to hand over the footage from the night of Amelia's disappearance and I found footage of her talking to a guy at the bar. He passed her a business card with that name on it and then a few minutes later she left with him."

"This could be what we've been missing." Jacquie's tone rose with excitement.

"I didn't actually see them leave the bar. But that could just mean they avoided the exterior cameras."

"Or he used magic to conceal their getaway. Herrera did say they suspected the ring of using magic to lure and control these women."

"Jonathan insists he would have known if someone was using magic in the bar."

"Did you get anything else useful out of Herrera? Like about our impending homicide victim?"

"Didn't get the chance. She said Jamal was kind of the lynchpin for their whole investigation. But she kept digging even after he died, even when the brass told her to drop it."

Jacquie's lips quirked into a sad smile. "Reminds me of someone we knew."

"You know, she acted like she had no idea who Ezri was."

"She was important in our circle, but not everyone's."

"There's more she's not telling us," I sighed.

"I told you I'd answer your questions." Herrera's voice came from the doorway where the older agent now stood.

"Why was Jamal so important to this case?" Jacquie cut me off before I could speak.

"He'd gained the trust of some people we thought might be lower-level brokers in the ring. We thought he was being careful, but clearly someone found out he was working with us."

"We found a connection to Fletcher Talent Management," I interjected. "It's also here in the emails he was bringing to you the night of his murder. And they're linked to the most recent abduction, too."

"How do you know that?"

"I watched the footage." She didn't need to know just how up close and personal I'd gotten with it. "I'm not sure our abductor actually used magic to lure her. From what I could tell, he had an earpiece in. So, someone could have been feeding him lines to lure her away from the crowd."

"The name came up in our investigation, but we couldn't find any clear links to Dermott," Herrera said, shifting her weight from foot to foot.

"Why is this case so important to you?" I made sure to make clear eye contact, so she couldn't evade the question.

"Don't you want to stop human trafficking and sexual exploitation?" she countered.

"I'm all for putting dirt bags behind bars where they belong, but you said it yourself, you thought the case died with Jamal. Also you were told to drop it. Why didn't you?"

Agent Herrera stepped into the conference room until we were toe to toe. Her face was a study in stoicism until she let out a long breath. Her features crumbled and her shoulders sagged. "My younger sister was taken and sold."

"By Dermott?"

"No. But someone like him. She met a man while she was in high school. I tried to talk her out of seeing him, but she was always strong-willed. Telling her to do something almost guaranteed she did the opposite. But one day, she called me and I could tell she was scared. I heard men's voices in the background. They were selling her like livestock."

"What happened after that?" The words came out of my mouth in a whisper.

"The police took a report, but they weren't interested," she answered, unshed tears sparkling in her eyes. "I don't know, I thought maybe I might have a chance of finding her again if I could dismantle this network. Maybe someone would talk to save their own skin and I'd find a lead on Lupe."

"I am so sorry," Molly's voice filtered from in front of us just beyond the conference room door.

Herrera wiped at her eyes to compose herself before looking at Jacquie. "Your brother was a valuable asset and I thought of him as a friend. To know that he died because of the work he was doing for me, I will carry that burden for the rest of my life."

"My brother was trying to do something good. He might not have put on a badge, but he was trying to protect people. He made that decision. You didn't make him do anything he didn't want to." That sad smile returned. "You weren't the only one with a strong-willed sibling."

"We need to look deeper into Fletcher Talent Management," I said to fill the silence.

"They have an office downtown," Herrera answered.

"I'm betting they have offices in Philly and New York, too," Jacquie added.

"So, what, we think they're using this agency to select their targets and then use the lure of a contract to get them to leave with them?" Molly posed.

"It's as good a theory as anything," I replied.

Before anyone else could speak, Jacquie's phone buzzed with an incoming call. I spotted Neveah's picture pop up on the screen.

"Do you need to get that?" Herrera didn't know we'd gotten much of our initial information from a clairvoyant teenager.

Jacquie nodded and snatched up the phone, pressing it to her ear. "Neveah, is everything okay?"

Most teenagers weren't awake voluntarily at five thirty in the morning. Whatever Neveah replied on the other end of the call prompted Jacquie to pull the phone from her ear and tap the 'Speaker' button.

"Say that again."

"I saw that woman again. In an office or something."

"You're saying what you saw changed?" I blurted.

"I don't know. It's never been this mixed up before." Neveah's voice crackled over the line. "I think she was in the same clothes from the car."

"Neveah, did you see anything special or distinct about her clothes? A name, a logo, or something?" I interjected, hovering over the phone as if my proximity to the device would cause her to make a connection we needed.

"I think I saw something, but it was fast."

"Wake your brother up, tell him what you saw and send it to me," Jacquie instructed.

"They've never come like this before, Aunt

Jacquie." Neveah sounded far younger than her age in that moment. The fear in her tone clutched at my chest. Poor kid.

"I know you're scared but you're doing exactly what you're supposed to," Jacquie coached. "Now, get your brother and send me what you saw. I promise, we're doing everything we can to stop this from happening again."

"I'll try," Neveah whispered before ending the call.

"Someone want to fill me in?" Herrera looked pointedly at Jacquie.

"My niece sees visions. She saw Jamal's death and then the woman we're tracking down. Costanza Valez. Neveah saw her in a similar car crash yet to happen. My niece is the reason we know we've got less than forty-eight hours left to save this woman."

Herrera's brow furrowed. "And you're sure they are connected?"

"There is no logical reason she would see a vision of her dead father who is linked to this case and then this woman. They have to be connected," I answered.

Just then, Jacquie's phone pinged with an incoming text. She tapped the screen and pulled up a hastily sketched image on a piece of notebook paper. It looked like a stylized F, T, and M. I snatched up the first email I could find with the full signature line from Jamal's contact at the company.

I held up the image for Herrera to see and gestured to the one Troy had drawn. "Doubt they're connected now?"

"No." She sounded resigned.

Footsteps outside the conference room drew our attention and Duncan appeared looking more rested than all of us combined. If I didn't know better, I would have guessed he'd taken some of J.T.'s pills.

"What did I miss?"

"Everything," I quipped.

Herrera cleared her throat and took a step toward the doorway. "I need to brief my team on what we've learned."

"You aren't going to Fletcher Talent Management without us."

She eyed me and shook her head. "No, of course not. But we need to divide and conquer if Agent DeWitt's niece is right on the timeline. We need to find the missing link between Dermott and Fletcher. If he's really using it to funnel women into his pipeline, we need ironclad proof."

She stepped past Duncan and disappeared from view. Molly fixed him with an expectant look. Molly wasn't surprised at all to see him rolling in late to the party.

"Jamal was in correspondence and dealing with a company called Fletcher Talent Management. Looks like their offices don't open until eight o'clock," Molly explained.

"And Herrera's team is looking for a link between them and our kingpin," Duncan recapped. "How do we know they're involved in Amelia's disappearance?"

"I saw it on the video footage we got from Notre Dame," I answered.

"Wow, you must be growing on him," he laughed.

I glanced in Molly's direction. "I think name-dropping his girlfriend might have put him in a more cooperative mood."

She smirked and shook her head. "He really is coming around to law enforcement, I swear he is."

"That will be the day," I snorted. "But on a related note, has he ever told you about what kinds of wards he keeps up around the place to deter magic use inside?"

"We don't really talk shop." Molly's cheeks flushed a rosy shade of pink.

"I don't remember him having anything back when we were crossing paths more often," I said.

"Uh, it happened after the kidnapping case," Molly explained.

"Hmm ... After Lola's pyro pal nearly set the bar on fire." Jacquie almost sounded amused.

"That was one hell of a night," Molly added.

"So, a relatively recent change," I noted. If there really were wards inhibiting magic, that explained the strange feeling I'd gotten at the bar the other night. And why the groper had looked so strained. "Someone was feeding our guy information. I spotted him tapping his ear a couple times while he was talking to Amelia at the bar. But there was no audio in the recording."

"You think whoever was helping him out knew they couldn't use magic inside?" Duncan suggested.

"Maybe. A lot of people come through the bar. Honestly, it isn't a big secret Jonathan doesn't like power being flung around inside, even before these wards went up. But it's also no secret that people with magic go there. I don't know, maybe they were hoping to find some more people to recruit for them?"

"Did you ever get a chance to check with the

Council about our missing women?" Jacquie interjected.

"Not yet. J.T. was floating the idea yesterday. But I can go nudge him. Maybe the Council will have something on Dermott."

"I know it's early, but go pay him a visit. We don't have time to waste," Molly directed. "Take Duncan."

"Yes, ma'am," I replied.

Duncan was quiet on the way down in the elevator. As the floors ticked by overhead, I couldn't help but reflect on our first meeting when he'd greeted me on the tarmac and then again when we'd ridden up together for the first time. I'd sensed he was someone I could trust and rely on, and ever since he hadn't given me any reason to doubt that assessment

"What did she have you doing?" I demanded as the elevator doors slid open.

"I don't know what you're talking about," he denied and stepped into the lobby.

"No, you don't get to do that. I saw that look she gave you. You had a reason for being late. What's going on?"

"She had me pay a visit to an old acquaintance of hers to see if they knew anything about Dermott."

"What acquaintance?"

"Uh ... that guy, Taggart."

"He's a dirty cop and a murderer. I wouldn't trust a word that comes out of his fucking mouth," I snapped. "I told you he used Kevin to do his dirty work."

"I get it, trust me. I took no pleasure in it. But he actually had some pretty interesting things to say. I'll fill you in on the drive."

TWELVE

I kept my mouth shut until we were in the car before the words erupted out of me. "I can't believe she sent you to see that bastard. When did you even find the time?"

"While you and Herrera were at the bar, Molly arranged a special late night visit," Duncan explained and pulled into the very beginnings of rush hour traffic.

"She could have told me," I muttered.

"And have you react exactly like this?" he retorted. "Kayla, I understand you have strong feelings towards that guy. And believe me, I got slime ball vibes off him the moment I walked into the room, but you didn't see the way he reacted when I mentioned Dermott's name."

"Tell me what he said."

Before answering, he eased to a stop at a red light. "I will, but first I need to know where we're going."

I blinked at hm in confusion for a moment before realizing I'd been operating off the assumption J.T. would be at Authority Headquarters. But it was coming up on six o'clock in the morning and he was still a working paramedic. One whose shift schedule I didn't know.

"Right," I mumbled and pulled up Avery's number to hit the call button.

"Hello?" she answered sleepily after the fourth ring.

"Hi, sorry to wake you up, but do you know if J.T. is working today?"

I heard the rustle of bedsheets and blankets. "I don't know. But I have his number, hold on."

"Thanks. I appreciate it," I said as my phone dinged with an incoming text. I checked the screen before saying, "Got it."

Switching calls, I waited as J.T.'s line rang. He answered on the second ring. "J.T. Somers."

"Hey, J.T., it's Kayla. Sorry if I woke you up."

"Oh, hey. No, I was up."

"I hate to bother you, but we've got some new

information on the case and hoped you were up to doing a little digging through files at Authority Headquarters?"

"I put the word out yesterday after we talked and I have the electronic ledger of Authority members. No need to go all the way out there."

"Great. Where do you want to meet?"

"You can come by my place. I'll text my address."

"We'll be there in twenty," I replied and ended the call. At least I knew where to direct Duncan.

I plucked his phone off the holder on the dashboard and input J.T. 's address before securing it again. "We have directions now. What did that asshole say?"

"The minute I dropped Dermott's name, he got this look like I'd said the most offensive thing in the world. He wanted to know where I'd heard the name."

"Please tell me you didn't give him sensitive case information."

"I told him he was a person of interest in an active investigation. He specifically name-dropped Agent Herrera, calling Dermott her white whale."

I was about to ask how he even knew about Herrera before I remembered he'd been an FBI agent for years before I'd come on the scene. "Did he give you anything useful? Anything we couldn't find out on our own?"

"After I clued him in that I knew about magic, he couldn't talk fast enough. According to Taggart, Dermott started out within the ranks of the Order of Samael, but it became clear pretty quickly that what interested him was well beyond what the rest of their group of lunatics were comfortable with."

"Ezri always said that the Order just wanted to use their magic for their own purposes. No rules or oversight," I added.

"Yeah, well apparently Taggart was around when Dermott broke away from the Order. It was kind of a big shake up at the top of the organization."

"Did he have any information on whether he's linked to Fletcher?"

"He confirmed that Dermott's big thing was using magic to compel people to do what he wanted, so it certainly sounds like the methods Herrera described."

"We already know he's a sick bastard. We need something we can actually use to nail him for this."

"He did mention something about Dermott having a cousin that owned some sort of business. Taggart suspected it was involved in his schemes."

"Did he happen to name this cousin?'

Duncan quirked a half-smile at me. "Madison Fletcher."

That was something we could use. I hit Jacquie's number on speed dial. "You by a computer?" I asked when she answered the call.

"Yeah, what did you find?"

"I need you to run the name Madison Fletcher through our databases. Taggart thinks he's related to Dermott. It could explain why they're using the agency as a front to lure their victims."

"Give me a minute."

I could hear her typing over the line and I waited impatiently as Duncan followed the GPS to J.T.'s place.

"Okay, here we go. Madison David Fletcher is the President of Fletcher Entertainment Holdings. It looks like Fletcher Talent Management is a subsidiary."

"Any familial connection to Dermott?" I pressed.

"Let me see what else I can find on this guy. I'll get back to you," Jacquie said and hung up.

Duncan glanced at me again as we eased to a halt at a stop sign. "Taggart did tell me one other thing before I left last night."

My stomach did an involuntary flip. "What?"

"He told me if we could actually nail Dermott,

then there might be some actual justice in the world."

"Taggart's a murderer and a traitor to the badge he wore. He doesn't get to claim that what 'we' are doing is justice," I spat, placing emphasis on the word 'we.'

"Maybe not. But I looked at his record before everything hit the fan a few years ago. He was actually making a difference. Seemed like he specialized in white collar stuff."

"Putting away some rich white boys isn't going to earn him any points," I answered.

"I'm just saying people are complicated and maybe he's trying to make up for his past now?"

"He only does what's good for him."

"Tell me something. What are you hoping to find with J.T.?"

"I don't know, some sort of pattern?"

"And what if none of the victims actually have magic?"

"I don't know. Maybe we're chasing a dead end. But don't we owe it to these women to try?" I snapped.

"Of course, we do."

"I can't shake this feeling that Constanza is familiar. The name isn't, but there's something about her picture. It's like right on the edge of my brain, but I can't catch hold of it ... what if I remember it too late?"

"We still have a day and a half. We're going to save her," Duncan said.

"So, you can see the future now too?" I hadn't meant the words to come out so harsh. Pinching the bridge of my nose, I sucked in a breath and held it for a ten count. "It's Jacquie's family and they deserve closure. I mean, I just feel like there's so much riding on this and I don't want to screw it up."

"This isn't all on you, Kayla. It never has been. No one expects you to be amazing at this. You graduated top of your class, that's great. But that doesn't mean you have to be perfect."

I knew he was right. Yet, deep down, I still felt this nugget of guilt; this feeling that I was only pretending and playing at being a hero. In reality, I was just some loser who could barely keep hold of her magic on a good day. The girl who walked through walls and hid from the world, because it was easier than dealing with my own shit.

"Guess I've been having some imposter syndrome lately," I offered softly.

"You've helped us crack this thing. Without you we would have never gotten those files from Jamal's car. And we wouldn't have been able to identify Constanza to know she was in danger."

"Neveah did the heavy lifting," I reminded him.

"Don't sell yourself short," he countered as we pulled into a spot outside of J.T.'s building.

I climbed out of the passenger seat and headed to the front door, which unlocked with a buzz before I had a chance to ring the bell. Duncan trailed me up to the apartment. J.T. stood in the doorway wearing jeans and a t-shirt.

"Thanks for helping us," I told him as he let us in.

"I'll be honest, it's not the way I thought I'd ever be helping the magical community. But if it makes a difference, I'm for it."

"Hey, can I float a couple of names by you?" I looked at J.T. as he gestured to a laptop that sat waiting on the living room table.

"Sure."

"Does the name Constanza Valez ring any bells? She might have started coming to Authority Head-quarters recently."

"No, but let me check the ledger," he said and bent over the keyboard. "Sorry, that name doesn't come up. We don't even have anyone with the same last name."

"Would you have anything on people who were members of the Order?"

J.T. sighed. "I wish. I mean we had some names we've kept from Ezri's old cases, but we don't have anything close to a complete record."

"So, there's nothing in there about Nathanial Dermott? He would have splintered off years ago."

His brow creased and he returned his attention back to his computer. He tapped away at the keys, but whatever information filled his screen wasn't what he'd hoped for. "The name comes up as once associated with Reuben Wickham. But nothing in the last few years."

Reuben Wickham, the man responsible for Neveah's kidnapping two years ago. Also, one of the Order's higher-ups who'd had their magic stolen and their memory of all magic erased.

"What about Madison Fletcher?" It was an even bigger long shot, given the fact Taggart had confirmed that Dermott was involved with the Order. If Fletcher was in fact related and helping his cousin's shady dealings, it was unlikely he'd be in the Authority's ledger.

"That's interesting," J.T. murmured, pulling the computer on his lap, and sinking into the couch behind him.

I was at his side, peering over his shoulder in seconds. Madison's name, along with two others—Stacy and Patricia—appeared in the ledger as having been Authority members. The last recorded date they'd engaged with anyone from the organization was six years ago.

"What is it?" Duncan remained by the door.

"Madison and his family look to have been a part of the Authority for a while, but they fell off the map around six years ago."

"That's around the time Jamal was involved with the investigation," Duncan confirmed.

"Is there any other information you can find about Stacy or Patricia? Ages, or what they look like?" I had to stop myself from reaching for the laptop myself.

"Looks like Stacy and Madison were married. I see a maiden name of Crowne for her, but Patricia shares the same last name as Madison. Looks like, at least six years ago, Patricia was in her late teens."

I pulled out my phone and did a web search for Madison Fletcher. An image popped up of a man with a tanned complexion and short-cropped hair. He was smiling for the camera, arms wrapped around two women, who I guessed were his wife and daughter. The younger woman wore long sleeves despite the fact her parents were in a short-sleeved shirt and sleeveless dress. I noticed a pinched look on her face, too. It was a look I'd seen before on people trying to hide their addiction while I'd been living with Lola.

"Was Denise DeWitt on the Authority ledger back then?" The pieces were starting to click into place. At least a picture was forming in my head that made sense.

"Yeah, although she wasn't active much around then. It wasn't until a few years ago thanks to Gabby and Carly that Neveah got involved in training. And honestly, I'm pretty sure that was all thanks to Jacquie."

"Do you think the two could have crossed paths? I mean, I know you guys have healing lessons, but did anyone ever run anything like support groups out of the building?"

"Like for addiction?"

I nodded.

"Not that I can remember, but to be honest, I was focused mostly on getting used to being a full-time paramedic back then. I wasn't around nearly as much as I am now."

"Thanks. This has been a big help," I said, pushing myself to my feet.

"Wait, I thought you wanted to run a bigger list by me?" J.T.'s hands sat poised over the keyboard ready.

"Email me a copy of the ledger and we'll have someone cross reference for us. I should have just done that from the beginning. Sorry to take up your time but we need to get back to the office." I was halfway to the door already.

"Sure, no problem." I caught the look of bewilderment on J.T.'s face as I pulled the door open and stepped into the hallway, motioning for Duncan to follow me.

"Okay, what the hell was *that*?" Duncan demanded once we were back on the street.

Before I could launch into an explanation, my phone buzzed with an incoming text from Jacquie. I pulled it up and showed it to Duncan. **'Taggart was right. Dermott and Fletcher are first cousins on their mothers' sides.'**

"We'll need to dig into Fletcher's family. But we know that back then, Denise struggled with addiction," I began and gestured for the keys. He tossed them overhand at me before I slid behind the wheel, pulling the address for Fletcher Talent Management's Boston office. "I know it's speculation right now, but what if Fletcher's daughter was an addict, too."

"Okay, so maybe they knew each other. So?"

"Can you pull up Jamal's case file? I need Denise's phone number," I said, ignoring his question.

To his credit, Duncan did as I asked and even dialed Denise's number. It rang five times, then six. This was not the kind of question I wanted to ask over a voicemail.

"Hello? Who is this?" Denise finally answered just before it clicked to voicemail.

"Denise, this is Kayla Rogers. I work with Jacquie," I said as Duncan held the phone up, so I could speak into it.

"What do you want? Haven't you traumatized my daughter enough?"

"I'm really sorry for everything Neveah's been going through. But I actually had a question for you."

"I told Jacquie I can't talk about what happened to Jamal."

"I understand. I just need to know if you ever met someone named Patricia Fletcher."

"Why are you asking about Patti?"

I glanced at Duncan and he gave me an approving nod. "Because I think she might be connected to what happened to Jamal. I know it's painful to talk about, but can you tell me how you know her?"

"We met in an N.A. group a few years ago. She struggled to cope with the pressure of her rich father. You wouldn't think we had much in common. Until we realized we both had gifts."

"Did Jamal ever meet her?"

"A couple times when he came to pick me up from meetings. It wasn't like they socialized."

No, but if he'd heard his wife's friend was in danger of relapsing, he might have gone to try offering help and money to get her off the street.

"If she were going to relapse, do you know where she'd go to score?"

"Downtown, near Copley Square. What is going on?"

That wasn't far from where Jamal had been arrested on solicitation charges. "I can't share anything more, but you've been really helpful, Denise. Thank you. I promise we're going to put this all to rest and you and your family can finally move on."

I motioned for Duncan to end the call. "Herrera and her team must have already gotten wind of the fact that Fletcher might have been involved with

Dermott. Or at the very least known about their familial connection. If Patricia's name ended up in a police report for solicitation, it might explain why they swooped in and brought Jamal onboard."

"You think someone on her team knew about the magical connection? Might have even used that as leverage to get Jamal's cooperation."

"Very possible. Things are finally starting to make sense."

"One thing I don't understand is how could Dermott have been in the car with Jamal and then not?" He held up a hand before I could answer. "And please don't say magic."

I had been so focused on what lay ahead of us, I hadn't been focusing on the past. I knew magic could do a great many things, but making someone a shadowy essence was not something I'd ever seen before.

"If we knew how powerful Dermott was, it might help explain what he was able to do. I'm starting to think what Neveah saw in her vision was more an interpretation. Like he wasn't actually there in the car with Jamal. If I had the time, I could have tried to go back into my own memory of what I'd seen to confirm whether there was another reflection in the rearview mirror."

"What, he astral projected into the car?"

"Maybe. If he's powerful enough, then I bet he could have accomplished that." Besides, even if he wasn't that powerful, there were ways he could change that, like taking magic from other people. It was unpleasant and either left their victims with a gaping hole in their soul, or no memory of magic ever existing. Neither option thrilled me.

"Isn't knowing he was behind it enough?" I added as the theater district came into view, the downtown Boston skyline catching the early morning sunlight off upper-level windows.

"What about Constanza? We know that Dermott is going to take the same approach with her if we can't get to her in time."

"So, if we find her, we don't let her get in a car alone," I answered with a shrug.

"For someone who was touting imposter syndrome not an hour ago, you seem awfully confident in your ability to take on some unknown level of magic all by yourself."

"Maybe your little pep talk had an effect on me. I'm trying to believe that we'll succeed. Freaking out about whether I was doing this right wasn't helping, so why not try manifesting what I want to happen."

The stylized F, T, and M came into view. I

pulled into a vacant spot on the side of the street. "We probably shouldn't announce we're FBI right off the bat. We don't want to spook Fletcher," I said.

"As much as I want to disagree, you're not wrong. And while I would love to say I'm model material, I think you've got me beat in that department," he noted.

Embarrassment warmed the nape of my neck. I gave a curt nod, accepting the compliment and climbed out of the car, setting my badge, and gun in the vehicle. "You know, maybe you ought to come up, just in case." Though I'd only been carrying the badge and weapon a short time, I already felt at a disadvantage without them, even with magic at my disposal.

"You got it, partner."

We headed inside and up to the fifth floor. The plush burgundy carpeting muffled our approach to the door with a frosted glass window sporting the same logo as the exterior of the building. I slid out of my suit jacket and undid a button or two of my blouse. I wanted to look professional, but not scream 'cop.'

My phone buzzed with an incoming call from Molly, but I silenced it. The clock was ticking and I needed to focus on why we'd come here. I eased the door open and stepped into an office with calming yellow walls, plush chairs, and a couch. The same carpeting extended into this room from the hallway to muffle my steps. A sturdy desk sat at one end of the room bearing the identification Receptionist. The chair behind the desk was vacant, but I could hear voices from behind another interior door. The reception area was devoid of any other people waiting to be seen. That was a point in our favor at least. I spotted a tiny silver bell on the counter and rang it. It gave a soft 'ding.'

"Coming," a surprisingly familiar voice called.

The interior door opened and the woman whom Avery had identified as Constanza Valez appeared. Except up close, I could spot the dye job and the fake nose piercing. Our gazes met and her mouth dropped open. Constanza Valez was no practitioner. She was Special Agent Perri Frasier.

THIRTEEN

How could I be so stupid? We'd spent so much time together; I should have been able to pick up on the ways she was disguising herself. We hadn't talked much in the last two months. We'd meant to keep contact, but our lives had gotten too busy, located in different cities. I'd never considered the silence on her end came from her being on assignment in my own backyard.

"What are you doing here?" Perri whispered.

"Looking for Constanza Valez," I countered, arms crossed over my chest.

"You can't be here right now," she said, glancing nervously over her shoulder at the door she'd come through.

"You're working with Philomena Herrera," I said before she motioned for me to keep my voice down.

"Please, you need go."

"No. I'm not leaving my friend in a situation that is giving me bad vibes." I pointed to the door leading to the hallway. "Just come with me, for a few minutes. Please."

Perri looked at me, glanced at the door again and nodded, stepping around the desk. We stepped outside of the receptionist area onto the carpeting to find Duncan looking at his phone, his thumbs poised over the screen mid-text. I cleared my throat to get his attention.

"Molly called, she got some new information," he said before his gaze settled on Perri.

"Like the fact Constanza is actually an under-cover agent?" I hissed.

"How did you know?"

"It turns out we know each other," I answered.

"We can't be having this conversation here," Perri interrupted. "I need to get back in there before they realize I'm gone." She started back toward the door.

"You're not safe," I blurted.

That stopped Perri in her tracks. The color in her

cheeks drained as she looked from Duncan to me and back again.

"What do you mean?'

"We could explain if you just came with us."

"I can't just leave. But I go on break at ten for twenty minutes."

I wanted to tell her we didn't have the time to wait around. Except I also knew she was stubborn and there had to be a good reason she couldn't leave right now.

"I don't know what Herrera's got you doing, but whatever it is, you need to wrap it up," Duncan added. "Kayla's not wrong. You are in danger."

"Until I hear it from her directly, I'm not deviating from protocol," Perri said and disappeared back inside.

Before the door closed, I caught sight of two men coming through the interior doorway. One looked like the photo of Madison Fletcher I'd found online. The other was a tall, balding man who I had to assume was Dermott.

"Who were you talking to?" Dermott demanded, towering over Perri.

"Some girl came in asking about representation, but I knew she wasn't right for the brand. Not the right look," Perri lied.

"You're the help. You don't know what the right look is if it slapped you in the face," Dermott scoffed.

My hands balled into fists before I realized I had the urge to slug the prick for insulting my friend.

"Nate, be reasonable. I've given Constanza very clear instruction on what we're looking for. If she says the girl wasn't right, she wasn't right," Madison said.

It would be so easy to slip through the door unseen and record the conversation, but I knew that wouldn't hold up in court. And if we were going to dismantle Dermott's network, we had no room for error.

"Come on," Duncan hissed in my ear.

We retreated to the car and I dialed Herrera's number. She answered on the first ring.

"Please tell me you have not made contact."

"Too late. You knew her alias the moment I mentioned it. You knew she was in danger and didn't do anything," I said, anger bubbling in my throat.

"Agent Frasier is an asset and she needed to stay in place as long as possible, gathering information under the radar."

"Perri is my friend." After a beat, I added, "Does she know about the magic involved?"

"She was fully briefed before she went undercover."

I suddenly picked up ambient noise in the background as Herrera put the call on speaker on her end.

"Did she know about Jamal?" Jacquie's voice came over the line.

"You all can be mad at me later, but Agent Frasier is close to getting what we need to take this son-of-a-bitch down."

"What makes you think it's going to stick this time? We know Dermott was responsible for Jamal's death, but we can't prove it in a court of law. And did you miss the part about Neveah seeing Perri about to suffer the same fate in less than twenty-four hours?" My voice rose to the point I was shouting by the end.

"Agent Rogers, you need to get ahold of yourself," Herrera ordered.

I wanted so badly to end the call. Or worse, tell her to fuck off and let me save my friend's life. I did neither. It wouldn't accomplish anything productive, even if it would assuage my anger.

"Kayla, you need to stand down. Just for now." Molly's voice was gentler, less authoritative and yet it eased a little of the fire burning in my belly.

"Understood," I said. I ended the call, tossing the phone on top of the dash and let out a heavy sigh.

"Her break is only a couple hours away," Duncan noted.

"That's a couple of hours we could have gotten her the hell away from those psychos."

"We'll get her. We just have to be patient."

I WAS CRAWLING out of my skin by the time ten o'clock rolled around. I scanned every face leaving the Fletcher building, each time disappointed when Perri didn't materialize. I tried not to let panic get the better of me. I could hear the tiny voice in the back of my head taunting me that I'd missed something and she'd been found out. That they weren't going to bother trying to make it look like an accident. Finally, she appeared through the revolving door and headed up the street away from us.

"We have to go after her," I said, reaching for the steering wheel in an effort to get Duncan moving.

"It would be too obvious if we followed right now," he said.

Before I could argue with him, my phone buzzed with an incoming call. It skittered across the top of the dash and I caught it just as it fell toward my feet. A number I didn't recognize flashed on the screen and I scrambled to answer.

"Hello?"

"I'm sending you a pin. Come meet me. I don't have a lot of time."

A few seconds later, my phone dinged with the alert that I'd received the pin drop on my map app. "We'll be right there."

Duncan put the car in drive and pulled into the flow of traffic, following the tiny red dot on the map to a small park with a smattering of benches. Perri sat under the shade of one of the few trees in the area.

I could see her training kicking in as she scanned the area behind us, checking to see if we were followed. There was a reason she'd been tapped for undercover work.

"I heard from Herrera. She told me you've been read in on the case." Perri spoke quickly, a nervousness in her tone that threw me.

"That's why we're here. We have credible information that Dermott is going to come after you. Five years ago, he killed an informant and we believe he's going to try to do the same to you. Make it look like an accident."

"I knew this job would be dangerous," Perri murmured.

"You don't have to go back. Just come with us to FBI headquarters. We can debrief, come up with a new plan of attack," I begged her.

"You don't understand. There are files I need to get on a flash drive in my desk. I will go with you, but I have to retrieve it first."

I wanted to tell her to forget the drive, let it get swept up in any search that was initiated. Except I realized whatever information she had on the drive likely was the probable cause Herrera would need for any search warrants.

"Is Dermott still there?"

"How did you know ..." She trailed off.

"You left the door open and he has a big mouth," I said.

"I thought it might have been magic."

My gaze narrowed at her. "How did you find out?"

"You were read in on our file. She filled me in on you."

"She didn't have a right to tell you that."

"It's pretty damn relevant, Kayla."

"Not that this isn't an important issue that should be discussed at a later time. But maybe we should get back to finding the best way to get Agent Frasier out of there with the evidence she needs as quickly as possible?" Duncan interrupted.

"Where is it exactly?"

"It will be faster if I go. It won't arouse suspicion that way."

"If she told you I've got magic, then she probably let you know that I can basically walk through walls. I could be in and out unseen."

"Or Kayla goes in as unseen back-up and takes the drive out," Duncan suggested.

"Fine," Perri sighed. "And no, Dermott shouldn't be there. He only comes by once a week to check on things. He usually leaves right after they meet I think he's been doing something to Mr. Fletcher."

"Like what?"

"I don't know. But he always seems a little out of it after they meet."

If Dermott was using magic to control the women he trafficked, it would make sense he'd resort to similar tactics to get his cousin to fall in line and do as he's told.

"Okay, let's get this over with. But you have to promise me, whatever you do, do not get in a car for the next two days okay?"

"I'll try," Perri answered and checked the time on her phone. "I need to get back."

"Meet you there."

I outpaced Duncan on the walk back to the car. He caught up to me at a jog. "You need to be careful. You don't know what this guy is capable of."

"I'll be fine," I said, brushing off his concern, if only to reassure myself that I could do this. Besides, I had someone to fight for and there was no chance in hell I would let this prick take my friend from me.

I caught sight of Perri heading through the revolving door and followed her at a safe distance. I even let her take the elevator up before catching the next one. But she waited for me outside the office.

"You better do whatever it is you need to do," she whispered.

My magic, fueled by my need to keep my friend safe, leapt to attention and turned me incorporeal with barely any effort. I heard Perri gasp as I vanished from sight. Duncan appeared from one of the other elevators, hanging back.

"I'll be right behind you," I said to Perri.

"So freaky," she muttered, but reached for the door handle.

"You should probably let Herrera and everyone

at headquarters know what's going on," I told Duncan.

"You thinking we might need some back-up?"

"Better to be overprepared."

I fell into step behind Perri as she moved across the hallway carpeting into the reception area. It was eerily quiet. I would have thought there would be people waiting for appointments. At least on the outside, the agency looked to do legitimate business. It wouldn't be a good cover otherwise. I stepped out of the way, so she wouldn't risk running into me as she shut the door.

Perri glanced toward the interior door as she reached into the bottom drawer of the reception desk. I could see the tremor in her hand as she pulled out a tiny flash drive. She started to raise her hand, but stopped mid-gesture. If anyone happened to walk through either door, they would find a truly bizarre scene.

So, I stepped up to the desk and slid my hand across the papers laid out neatly on top of the large monthly calendar. She picked up on the cue and laid the drive down just behind the name plate. I scooped it up and pocketed it, the dark plastic drive vanishing along with the rest of me.

Perri's shoulders relaxed a little as she sat down

in her chair. Now I just had to make my exit. I headed for the door, intent on walking right through it. Instead, I slammed into the frosted glass. I staggered back, trying to regain my balance as Perri uttered, "Oh, shit."

"Wha—" It dawned on me too slowly. I glanced down to find myself fully visible and a throbbing ache in my head confirmed I had in fact slammed face first into the door.

I didn't have time to react as the interior door to the office slammed open and Nathaniel Dermott's hulking form materialized above me. I blinked black spots from my vision just in time to feel a wave of energy smack me back into one the couches.

"You think I'm an idiot? That I wouldn't be prepared for some pretty witch with magic to come after me?"

He'd put up wards to neutralize magic that didn't benefit him. *Had he known I was coming after all?* He'd allowed me to use my own magic as a way to make me believe I had the upper hand. If I'd bothered to do any reconnaissance I would have realized that there were wards and taken precautions. I'd been so focused on getting Perri out of there, I hadn't stopped to think what defenses he might have thrown up.

"What are you doing?" Perri demanded, trying to put herself in his path.

"Out of my way you little spy," he snarled and physically flung her against the nearest wall like a rag doll.

She crumpled into a heap, the loud 'thwack' of her head hitting the wall reverberating in my ears. I pushed myself to my feet, seeing my friend injured spurring me on.

"It's over, Nate," I spat, planting my feet, readying myself for the next onslaught.

"You think you know anything, bitch?" he laughed.

I could hear his voice echoing in my head as I pictured the fear in Jamal's eyes the night he died. He had already shown he didn't need to touch someone to hurt them. "I know that you murdered Jamal DeWitt five years ago, because you thought he was snooping in your business."

"What proof do you have?

"Oh, I can't get you for that. Believe me, I wish I could. I have a friend who would love to put the bracelets on you for his murder. But I know you've been exploiting the young women coming through these doors. Exploiting your cousin, too, I bet."

"You have it all figured out, don't you?"

He didn't give me a chance to respond before he balled his hand into a fist and the air squeezed out of my lungs. I clutched at my throat, but it was rebelling against my brain's need for oxygen. My vision greyed faster than I thought possible and darkened at the edges as he pushed my body closer to hypoxia.

"You know, I have a few friends up in Albany who would love to acquire a smart mouth like yours." Dermott laughed. "Ha, they would break you easily in hours, you'd be begging them for more. And you think your little magic trick of turning invisible is cute? We'd make you actually disappear."

'You are stronger than this asshole,' a surprising voice said from beside me.

I strained to see who had spoken, because it sounded a hell of a lot like Ezri. But she was dead and as far as I knew she wasn't haunting any of us. Was I that close to death that I could connect with her?

'Fight, Kayla. Be the badass punk chick who called me on my bullshit,' the voice continued to push.

My hands felt disconnected from the rest of me as I fought to bring them up to defend myself. I could almost feel Dermott's hands wrapped around my throat, but it was only a projection. That's what I'd seen in Neveah's vision. She hadn't understood what she was seeing and her young mind had substituted in what she thought made sense.

Chamomile erupted around me as if I'd dumped an entire tea shop of the stuff into the room. It cascaded across my skin, tangled in my hair and eyelashes, even coated my teeth and tongue. I bit my tongue to try and ground myself. The sharp pain and the taste of blood mingling with the scent of my power was the jolt I needed.

Get your murderous hands off me!

Dermott took a step back, surprise etched into his features. He wasn't used to people fighting back. Tough shit for him.

"You are going to prison for a very long time, Nate," I snarled. "You've got an old buddy there waiting to welcome you. Jamison Taggart. I think he'll be really happy to see you. I'd say some of your old Order pals would be there, too, but I guess I have to commend you for getting out before their plans to overthrow humanity went to shit and they ended up with no magic and no memory."

"Bitch, who are you? You think you're so smar—" Dermott raised his hands again, but I was faster this time.

I held my own hands up and envisioned him

immobile, his arms locked by his sides. On the far side of the reception area, Perri roused. Good, she would be okay. I could also pick out the sounds of muffled voices beyond the exterior door. Likely the team had come to back me up. Even though I didn't need their help.

"Enough talking now," I told Nate and his lips pressed into an immovable thin line. Panic set in on his face as he fought for shallow breaths through his nose. I closed the distance between us, anger coursing through me. "You scared? Feel helpless, like you don't matter?" I spat. "Good. That's exactly what each and every one of those women felt the moment you walked into their lives."

I tilted my hands upward and his feet lifted off the ground. I could almost see him smashing through the door behind him. It would be easy, he deserved the pain.

"Enough, you've proved your point," Perri said from her spot on the floor.

The door burst open behind me. I caught Jacquie and Molly leading the charge, weapons drawn.

"You good, Agent Rogers?" Molly's tone was stern.

"I'm fine," I answered, hands still raised.

"No one wants him to suffer more than I do,"

Jacquie said, lowering her weapon and moving into my field of vision. "But we do it the right way. Kayla, don't let him drag you down into the mud with him."

I blinked, my hands now shaking as I realized how far I'd been willing to go to make him suffer. It wasn't all about Perri either. I had wanted to hurt him for every life he ruined. The hundreds of women he'd ripped from their families.

Jacquie's hands pressed on mine, forcing them back to my sides. Dermott lowered to the floor and his body went lax. Molly was there to catch him, slipping handcuffs around his wrists. They glowed a faint blue for a moment and Dermott took on that pained expression I'd seen on the groper's face at the bar. *Did she have Jonathan ward the cuffs?* Clever. Agent Herrera moved past them, leading a few other agents into the back. They appeared moments later with a dazed looking Madison Fletcher in tow.

"Kayla, you did it," Perri said as Duncan helped her to her feet.

Out of the corner of my eye, I caught a flash of red. Maybe Ezri had been there or maybe it was just a hallucination. Either way, she'd given me one last push to get the job done.

"Yeah, we did."

AUGUST 12, 2019

Early afternoon sunlight struck the windshield as I pulled up to Notre Dame. I'd never come to the bar this early in the day. In fact, most days, it wasn't even open this early. The last time it was had been nearly two years ago for Ezri's wake. At least this time we weren't mourning a lost friend.

My head was still spinning from the confrontation with Dermott. I hadn't been sure I would be strong enough to take him down. Yet somehow I'd found the strength and control over my power to save my friend and myself. Perri's time undercover had been enough to gather the evidence Herrera and her team needed to connect Dermott to the trafficking network.

Madison had been more than willing to turn against his cousin. I hadn't had much time with him before other agents whisked him away for questioning. Though I got the feeling Dermott had used Patricia's addiction as a way in, taking the reins of the company, and even supernaturally influencing Madison to do as he was told.

"Earth to Kayla, you in there?" Duncan's voice sounded miles away.

I shook my head to clear my thoughts and he came into focus in the passenger seat. "Yeah, I'm good. Just relieved that's over."

"I know we're up in the air right now about going beyond work partners and friends, but I wanted to tell you how proud I am of what you accomplished yesterday."

"Thank you. That means a lot to me."

I knew it was killing him that we hadn't fully addressed what hung between us. I did like him and a part of me wanted to see where it went. But there was another part stuck in the past. I'd given Kevin the space he'd asked for, but maybe now, when things were finally settling down in my life, we could reconnect and see if there was anything there. Or, if were truly done then maybe I could actually move on.

"Let's go in," I said, feeling the awkward silence pressing in around me.

I was out of the car and into the evening heat before he could respond. The usual bouncer was missing in action. Despite that the front door was unlocked and sat ajar, inviting us in. The lack of a thrumming base was far more jarring than entering before the sun had gone down.

To my surprise, Molly stood behind the bar, passing out beers to everyone already assembled. Agent Herrera stood off to one side while Perri sat on a stool an arm's length from Molly. I joined Perri, wrapping an arm around her shoulders.

"I need to apologize for not letting you in on the whole magic is real thing before," I said, accepting the beer Molly passed me.

"You weren't in a place to share that part of yourself with me," Perri answered. "I have to admit, though, seeing you in action was absolutely badass and cements it in the history books, at least for me, that you are the best valedictorian to come out of Quantico."

I laughed. "I'm not sure I deserve that much praise. I'm just glad we could avert Neveah's vision. I'm not ready to lose any more friends to psycho assholes with a power complex."

"I'll drink to that." Perri clanked the neck of her beer bottle against mine and took a sip.

"I just want to say thank you for your assistance on finally putting this case to rest," Herrera interjected. "I know we didn't get off on the best foot, but without you, I don't think we would have succeeded."

"Did Madison really flip?" Duncan took a swig from his own beer.

"Gave us everything he had. Ledgers, information on real estate holdings, and shell companies. We have Dermott's entire network. Teams in New York and Philly are executing warrants as we speak."

"What about the women who were trafficked? Is there anything we can do to track them down?" The unspoken reference to her sister hung in the air between us.

"With the ledgers Fletcher turned over, we might have a good shot at bringing some of them home."

I looked around the space, noting Jacquie's absence. Molly set down her own drink. "Jacquie's spending the day with her family, finally putting Jamal to rest the way he deserves."

A sudden pang tightened my chest, hitching my

breath. "I realized there's something I need to do," I announced and tugged on Perri's arm. "Come with me."

No one argued as we bailed on the celebration, although I caught a wistful look in Duncan's eye. Perri didn't even ask where we were headed. Ten minutes later, we pulled up outside a cemetery. We walked through the main entrance and I led her to Ezri and Desmond's headstones.

"They're the reason I got my shit together and joined the academy," I explained. I gestured first to Desmond's grave. "He got me out of a bad situation and showed me what I could do with my magic if I wanted to help people."

"And her?"

"She was a pain in the ass and kind of a douche at first. But she grew on me. She was literally born to be the Savior and saved the world. Sometimes, I forget that I'm not them. That I wasn't born to be a hero. I'm just trying my best to follow in their footsteps."

"How did they die?" Her voice was soft, reverent.

"Line of duty, protecting magic. I know they're in my past, but I wanted you to understand what drives me. Because they were important to me and so are you. I never thought I would have so many people without magic to rely on."

Perri wrapped an arm around my shoulder and squeezed. "I'm glad to be part of your team, Kay. And you know, I'm thinking of putting in a transfer to Boston. I'm starting to like it here."

"I'm not sure this city can handle both of us together," I joked.

"For what it's worth, I think your friends would be proud of the way you handled yourself on this one. I owe you my life. That's not something I'm going to forget."

I hadn't set out to widen my circle of allies and share the secret of magic, my own included, with so many people. Yet it felt like the right call to make. I needed people to ground me and remind me what I was fighting for. Secrecy wasn't all it was cracked up to be.

QUICK AUTHOR'S NOTE

I WON'T LIE, this one took a lot longer to write than I'd hoped. I came into it knowing I wanted to explore Jacquie's past more, especially her relationship with her immediate family. That's where the impetus for the case originally started. I also knew I wanted the case bring up her brother's death because it was going to be a repeat event. But, as I was working through the story, I stumbled upon the idea that he'd been working with the FBI and he was killed to keep him quiet.

I enjoyed getting to see this new history for her and to have the other characters help her and her family heal and grieve this loss. This series has really been wish fulfillment for me as an author. I get to explore characters and stories that didn't make sense to fit in during Seasons of Magic and I am really excited to be building out the supporting cast around Kayla and company with Perri and Agent Herrera. I hadn't originally planned for Perri to make a reappearance in this book but when I realized we needed a second undercover agent in the storyline to have it all make sense, it seemed perfect. Kayla deserves a circle of people who understand her and support her. And I think I was as surprised as everyone else to see that little Ezri cameo near the end.

As I said, this trilogy has been about some wish fulfillment for me and the final book in the series is no exception. We've explored most of my favorites but there are tow that are still untouched (see what I did there ;)) and that means we get some more on Molly and Jonathan.

TURN *the page for a glimpse of Untouched Magic...*

<u>**UNTOUCHED MAGIC**</u>

The magic that defines us...

Kayla has finally settled into her life as an FBI agent and a witch. Still, when a day off leads her to magical explosion, she feels the pressure to be a hero, like her mentor.

Digging into the explosion leads her to a second crime scene with no obvious connections between the two. And when a third explosion at a local magical bar renders her powerless, Kayla is forced to rely on her wits and her team to chase down the clues to the who and why behind the attack.

As they begin piecing together the links in the chain of events, a heartbreaking motive emerges. With the clock running out, will Kayla diffuse the situation before everything she stands for goes up in smoke?

Read on for a glimpse at Kayla's final story.

ABOUT THE AUTHOR

Sarah Biglow is a *USA Today* bestselling author. She lives in Massachusetts with her husband and son. She is a licensed attorney and spends her days combatting employment discrimination as an Investigator with the Massachusetts Commission Against Discrimination.

You can find an up-to-date list of all my books here

9 781955 988230